FLESH AND BLOOD

François Mauriac

Translated by
GERARD HOPKINS

Carroll & Graf Publishers, Inc.
New York

First Carroll & Graf edition 1989
Reprinted by arrangement with Farrar, Straus & Giroux, Inc.

Carroll & Graf Publishers, Inc.
260 Fifth Avenue
New York, NY 10001

ISBN: 0-88184-533-7

Manufactured in the United States of America

To

FRANÇOIS LE GRIX

his friend

F. M.

I

CLAUDE FAVEREAU, after questioning the porters, had found the platform at last, where, well away from the main booking-office, the slow train, with its ancient rolling-stock, was standing in a siding, seemingly forgotten. He should have chosen the evening express, which would have landed him at Toulenne within three quarters of an hour, but, being a young man, had greatly preferred the afternoon train which would crawl along the banks of the Garonne, stopping at every station, as though the heat had slowed it down and forced it to wander through the orchards and the vineyards lying prostrate beneath the overpowering sun. At the endless stops he could hear, through the partitions, voices chattering away in the local dialect. At each of them the station-master walked along the train with a whistle in his mouth, and a look of importance on his face, because this was the supreme moment of his day. Claude loved these moments when there was nothing to stop him thinking of himself. He had not yet succeeded, never would succeed, in imposing order on his thoughts. Now that he was leaving the seminary for ever, he was in a state of inner confusion. He would never, he thought, lose this taste for mental withdrawal, this mania of self-examination, the gift which he had to perfection, of turning a third-class carriage into a monk's cell, an oratory. Self-communing had become almost a pleasure, and he was always impatient for the moment when he could indulge it. He longed to be alone with his thoughts, and had felt the pressure of that craving even while the abbé Floirac was standing by the carriage door engaging him in talk.

9

Obedient to the wishes of his masters, Claude had left the seminary without breathing a word of his intention to anyone except this one man who was his "official" friend. When it had to be decided who should be chosen to see him off, Floirac's name had occurred almost simultaneously both to him and to the Superior, though he knew perfectly well that the abbé was the last person in the world whom he would miss, and that he would have found it far more painful to say good-bye to fat old Parmentier, who was always bottom of every class, and enjoyed nothing so much as talking about pigeon-shooting, setters, and woodcock. Motionless on the dirty asphalte, the pockets of his soutane bulging with books, and every button-hole marked by a stain, Monsieur de Floirac talked, as he always had done on their walks together, about Father Tyrrel and the abbé Loisy. Did he realize that in six minutes' time the train would carry away finally and for ever the only one of his companions who had shown any real interest in the questions which endlessly fascinated him? Maybe he knew that he was a bad hand at putting his feelings into words, and that, no doubt, was why he filled the silences that fell between them, by summarizing the conclusions contained in an article which had been printed in the most recent issue of the *Revue d'apologétique*. The train began to move. For a moment Claude found himself thinking of his friend's lonely walk back. 'He will find comfort' he told himself, 'in metaphysical extravagances'.

The train pulled up at a suburban station, but only for a few moments. Providence, thought our traveller, had made a special point of seeing that he should be undisturbed. He was spared the invasion of some sun-hater who might have drawn the blind, and so deprived him of the companionship of this July day. He absorbed the heat with passionate ecstasy. They passed a holding where three chestnut trees showed as a single

dome of dense foliage. Time and time again, in the course of
the journey, he welcomed, as brothers, the motionless trees
with their smooth, cool trunks on which he would never lay
his hands. Already the uplands were coming into view, the
plain of the Garonne swelling into hills and basking in the
sweltering air.

As he looked at the familiar landscape, he turned his thoughts
to the life which he was leaving. Never again in the early
dawn would he go to chapel with psalms upon his lips. His
directors had insisted that he should give up all idea of the
priesthood . . . but, where his directors were concerned, it
was always he who had taken the lead, he who had drawn
from them the decision he had wanted. It was not that his
faith had been in doubt, nor that Monsieur de Floirac had
infected him with his own feverish worries about the author
of the Pentateuch or the Fourth Gospel. No, it was just that
shortly before his eighteenth birthday he had come to realize
the nature of his feelings, had been forced to recognize what
dangerous potentialities lurked within him. The theories held
by Monsieur de Floirac about the interpellation of *Tu es Petrus*
might leave him cold, but the poems of Lamartine and Hugo,
which he had read in the abbé Ragon's anthology, had set
loose in him a torrent of delight. A single day spent in the
country, lying on the sappy, springy grass, would induce in
him a dangerous languor which might last for a whole week.

It was then that, seeing his own predicament clearly, he had
spoken to Monsieur Garros, his director. "The time has gone
by" he had said, "of those romantic abbés, so much beloved
of Father Lacordaire and Father Gratry, those hearts which
were prepared to accept every sacrifice except that of being
loved no longer, and who, when they died – usually of con-
sumption – left a legacy of rather too emotional prayers . . .
I am terrified to think that I might become a René of the

priesthood at a time, when as curé in an industrial suburb, I ought to be a bone of contention between employers and trade-unions."

It was during the period of his military service that his eyes had been really opened, that he had come to see how inevitable it was that he should abandon all thoughts of a sublime vocation. Monsieur Garros had warned him against the coarseness he would find in barracks, and had predicted that his time with the Regiment would be a two-years' martyrdom. But the anticipated suffering had not come his way. His father had been foreman on the Lur estate, and he had early come to realize that the crudest sort of joke could produce in him an only too ready response. At first he had been careful not to laugh at the grosser indecencies. On night-marches, the songs sung to scraps of church music had, no doubt, made him acutely miserable: but he had very soon learned that no amount of obscenity could keep him from looking at the stars. 'It would be silly to pretend,' he had said to himself, 'that when we get back to quarters, and I can sit with a bottle in front of me, and a good hot stove at my back, I shall not feel a sort of animal satisfaction and a great surge of high spirits in no way different from those of my companions.' Looking back, he decided that the determining influences of youth, the promptings of flesh and blood, had taken hold of him and swept away the effects of his clerical training. His reading had merely served to clarify his mind. Thanks to it he could study with interested lucidity, the play and movement of his own lower instincts. . . .

Sometimes, on a Sunday, he had taken friends with him to Lur. He had a vivid recollection of afternoons spent in drinking white wine with his father and Abel, the cowman, all of them seated round a table marked with the rings left by glasses, in his mother's kitchen. On those occasions the gentle sound of Vesper bells had called to him in vain through the bright air, incapable of rousing him from his state of physical torpor behind the half-closed shutters.

Cadaujac, Podensac, Barsac, Preignac . . . the villages of the Gironde followed one another like strung beads along the river bank. Their tiny stations, all alike, stood quivering in the heat, and when the train drew out he could see little bare-footed urchins staring after it from under cupped hands. Claude let his eyes take their fill of the sulphurated vines, the crumbling walls, and the white roads striped with shadow. He took from his pocket the small round mirror which he had bought on manoeuvres, and straightened the knot of his red tie. At sight of his face which, from now on, was to be that of a man living in the world, he felt the wild happiness of a bird released from captivity – the same sort of happiness he had known in the army when his first Sunday leave came round. Ah! how terribly he had suffered at the thought of his denial, of the pleasure he had felt that no one now could point to him as being one of those who had been "also with Jesus of Nazareth". What a shameful delight it had been to sit down at a table in the company of soldiers and barmaids, and to realize that nobody could see in him the mark of those who had been with the Galilean! From now on he could give himself unreservedly to such pleasures. The rhythm of the wheels set him singing a mad, ridiculous song to a tune from Mehul's *Joseph*. . . .

It had been sometime before Monsieur Garros could be made to understand his reasons. At first he had dismissed them as absurd. It was difficult for him to resign himself to the necessity of losing a young man who was so vital a character that, compared with him, the other young clerics seemed dreary, and only half alive creatures. He would have liked to keep him for a further year after the completion of his military service. Claude could still remember the long months wasted in fruitless argument. In the smoke of his cigarette he could conjure up a picture of Monsieur Garros with his bony face which seemed to take up the minimum of space and, even at the most solemn moments, could not conceal a certain innate shrewdness, any more than his rather shapeless mouth could keep from smiling. To those eyes, to that mouth, Monsieur Garros owed a reputation for subtlety which he maintained by having always at his command a supply of stories which never failed to produce upon his audience the desired effect. This retailer of anecdotes, this traveller in clerical jocosities had, all the same a pious taste in human souls – though he handled them with clumsy fingers. Claude had a very clear recollection of the last assault he had had to endure – no longer ago than yesterday – and amused himself with rehearsing the dialogue which had taken place on that occasion.

"My son, I know that it is your wish to return to your father's house, and to make no further use of the intelligence with which God has seen fit to endow you. It is only right, however, that I should tell you of a proposal which has reached the Superior concerning you. It would be much to your advantage."

"Something, I suppose, to do with a tutorship?"

"Yes, my son."

"Please, Father, if you have any fondness for me, do not insist. You can't really want me to become the chattel of a strange family? I know that the death of the Marquis de Lur, who used me, during the holidays, for the cataloguing of his library, has left me with no alternative but to grow vegetables . . . but I am a great hand at that, besides, who knows, the new owner of Lur may let me go back to my beloved books. . . ."

According to Monsieur Garros, it would be foolish to count

on that. The new owner, Bertie Dupont-Gunther (of the firm
of Dupont-Gunther and Castagnède) was a self-opinionated
business-man who had not his equal for vulgarity in all
Bordeaux. He added to his other vices that of belonging to
the so-called Reformed Religion. . . .

"Although," Monsieur Garros went on, "he married a
Mademoiselle Casadessus – the daughter of an ancient Catholic
family of the Parish of Saint-Michel – his two children have
been brought up in heresy. I have even heard it said that his
wife died of sorrow and remorse. . . ."

But Claude was undaunted by the prospect of this monster
who, since he was kept all week in Bordeaux on business,
would spend only Sundays at Lur, and even that only in the
Summer.

Monsieur Garros fell back on weightier arguments:

"You will suffer, Claude: you will be constantly offended:
your feelings will frequently be hurt."

The young man could not help smiling now as he remembered the melodramatic outburst which he had inflicted on
Monsieur Garros: "Never let it be said that I blush for my
parents!" He looked down at his duck trousers and his large,
red hands. . . . Between Preignac and Toulenne the train
grew so excited that it actually took itself for an express – and
Claude found himself thinking of the Easter Week which he
had spent at Floirac with his friend. What agonies he had
endured on that occasion! At mealtimes, he had had to solve
the problem of forks and knives on the spot, under the eyes of
two young watchful misses ready to giggle at the first opportunity. There would be nothing of that kind to worry him in
his mother's kitchen. Besides, he counted on getting back to
the library, there to make himself drunk on books and dreams
and fancies. In the last resort, the church would always be
open, a place of delicious peace at the day's end, whither he

had never carried a wounded heart in vain. Perhaps he may even have been conscious of a hope at the back of his mind that his obscure existence at Lur might be merely a time of waiting: perhaps it occurred to him that life might seek him out upon his hill-top. With ears pricked for a summons, the nature of which he could not as yet imagine, he would hold himself in readiness. . . . He was not apprehensive about his parents. There would be but little talk between them, for there was not much to say. They had grown away from each other, though, like the Lur oaks, they were bound together by their roots.

Since this was a slow train, he had assumed that the station at Toulenne would be deserted, and indeed, all he saw on the sun-baked, fly-infested square, was his father's trap which was standing in the circular shadow cast by a round-topped acacia. Mignonne, the mare, was twitching her ears and her mule-like tail to keep the buzzing plague at bay. He noticed the black handkerchief which served his mother for a hat. She was sitting motionless, with her back to him. Old Favereau, collarless and with his paunch protruding above his trousers, took Claude by the shoulders and imprinted two smacking kisses on his cheeks, after which he went in person to look for the black trunk – like a servant's – which he carried out together with a portmanteau from the platform. Marie Favereau's greeting lacked warmth. She was less resigned than her husband to the idea of no longer being the mother of a priest, in whose house she had always hoped to spend an inexpensive old age, an object of respect to all her neighbours. She felt pretty certain that there was a woman at the bottom of this business. She had, however, promised not to be too sharp with the boy, and to give him time to think things over. Both she and her husband hoped that when Autumn came round they could persuade him not to waste all the book-learning he had acquired, but to turn himself into a gentleman.

Claude, perched on the back seat, was facing away from his parents. The road wound away from under the wheels of the trap like a yard-measure running out of its little box. In front of every door in Toulenne stood a heap of refuse in a cloud of flies. Women in petticoats, with untidy hair, were sitting on their doorsteps, separated from the passage within by tattered curtains. The suspension-bridge trembled as they passed over the roaring Garonne, where children were splashing in the old familiar spots. By this time Mignonne was moving at a slower pace, because the road led uphill. It was possible to talk. Dominique Favereau was not what might be called a great hand at conversation. His world was bounded by the vineyard in which he exercised authority over six men, two women, and four oxen, issuing his instructions in the tones of a man who had never forgotten the days when he was a sergeant-major in the army. When he had matters to discuss with Monsieur Gunther, he stood in the regulation attitude with his hands to his sides. His military stiffness enabled him to stand perfectly still and upright even when he had got three litres of white wine aboard. His right eye, which had once received a charge of buckshot, was permanently closed, though there were those who maintained that he could see out of it perfectly well when it suited him. But the other eye, a little bleary blob, devoid of lashes and eyebrow, took note of everything that went on at Lur.

As they slowly climbed the hill, Claude questioned his father about the new owners, but all he got for his pains was – "He's a hard man as hard men go, but not afraid of his workers – expects everything to be done just so – and knows the value of money." Claude did not expect to get much out of his mother, who was scarcely more talkative. The black handkerchief over her head made her look like one of those nuns whose coifs prevent one from ever guessing their age. Her narrow, wooden countenance was that of a woman who had long ago accepted silence and solitude as her fate. She lived on her memories of the two elder sons who had died, one at seven, the other at nine. Her peasant existence of hard work and loneliness gave her no chance to forget. For years now she had had only one ambition, to acquire perpetual ownership of a family grave where the two coffins might be laid. Not that communal graves were known in this part of the country. But for her those two coffins contained all that remained of her sons, and, though she told her beads regularly, and spoke of the Good God, she believed that they were in the earth, and nowhere else.

To make things easier for Mignonne, Claude climbed down from the trap. Looking at the couple who had given him birth, two black figures against the sky, he thought to himself (though with no intention of mockery) – "he's a tree, she's a hen". A puff of warm air, prelude of a storm, set three poplars trembling. At the bottom of the slope stood Saint-Macaire, already in shadow, grouped about the Romanesque church, which looked like a ship which had lain at anchor for centuries among the willows of the water-meadows. Claude was walking with his arms swinging free and his head slightly raised. The sound of bells from Viridis ahead was rich with the memories of childhood. They had a way of waking and tormenting him, especially at the oncoming of night. He could feel as a living, a continuing, reality the smell of the kitchen, and the cold touch of the tiled floor of the bedroom on his naked feet. Later on, the ticking of the clock and the sound of his father's snoring in the sleeping house would bring to the surface of his mind yet other submerged regions of his childhood.

The great trees of Lur held between their trunks the level beams of the dying day. Claude reflected that they also held

the still unknown destiny which had been awaiting him just
here from all eternity. . . . A pain, a joy beyond words to
express, was in the moving tops of the oaks. It seemed to be a
sign addressed to him. He felt, he saw confusedly, that the
calm of this lovely late afternoon, the tired oxen carrying back
a last load of sulphate, all these symbols of peace and serenity,
were the bearers of a lying message; that, perhaps, already, his
hour had struck.

The oil lamp shone down on the American cloth. The cuts
which Claude had made as a little boy still showed on it.
Abel, the cowmen, and his wife, Fourtille, asked in to do
honour to his homecoming, sat stiff and motionless before
their deep-bellied plates which Maria had filled to the brim with
a steaming soup smelling of spices and garlic, and strengthened
with lumps of bacon. Abel's moustache was dripping. He
might have been twenty-five; he might have been forty. He
was concentrating on his food with a look of intense serious-
ness. Suddenly his face assumed an expression of even more
compulsive greed. He announced that he was going to make
a "chabrot", and forthwith proceeded to pour the blood-red
wine into what remained of his soup, so that the crimson
surface was starred with greasy patches. Then, lifting the bowl
in two hands, he plunged his great hirsute muzzle into the
mixture. The splash of the descending broth was clearly
audible from within the powerful body round which there
hung a combined smell of livestock, human sweat, and earth.
He wiped his mouth with the back of a bare arm covered with
a mat of black hair, and sat back with a look of solemn expectancy on his face, waiting for the pickled pork that was to
follow.

Claude, who was feeling slightly dazed as a result of the
white wine and his flooding memories, pricked his ears to
catch what Fourtille was saying about the new masters.

According to her, Monsieur Dupont-Gunther was no better
than a monster whose wife had died of a broken heart . . . his
daughter, Mademoiselle May, was a "stuck-up piece". The
son, Edward, had not yet put in an appearance. . . . The
whole bunch of them were to spend July in the Great House,
and the housekeeper was arriving tomorrow, to get things
ready. . . . Claude did not much bother his head about these
folk with whom he hoped that he would have nothing to do.
By this time Abel and Favereau had lit their pipes. A haze of
smoke eddied about the hams suspended from the beams, the
pots of jam on the dresser, the fly-spotted trade Almanacs, the
framed school-certificates, and the First-Communion memen-
toes. Maria had washed up the dishes and arranged them on
the rack. Only Fourtille was still talking. She expressed
surprise that Claude should not make an effort to earn his
living by "book-learning", and wear a town suit and a bowler-
hat. Favereau, not wishing to have the subject discussed, said
to Abel:

"Did you see in the paper that some clever bloke in
Bordeaux has been and invented a new vine disease?"

Maria, sitting bolt upright in a low chair, was busy with her
knitting. A puff of night air from the open door set the lamp
flaring. Moths were staggering about on the table-top.

"I'm going out for a breath of air," said Claude. There was
no moon, and it was pitch-dark outside. Nothing could be
seen but the distant lights of Toulenne, and a long snake of
flame from a train crossing the viaduct. The shrilling of
cicadas was so continuous that Claude soon ceased to be
conscious of it. From the invisible ponds came a loud croaking.
He could have found his way along the paths with his eyes
shut. He had a feeling that the trees had known him for a very
long time, and were drawing aside so that he should not bump
against their trunks, on which, in the old days, he had so often

leaned his forehead. The stones of the terrace were still warm to the touch. Now and again there was a sudden rustle of branches. There, in the concourse of his unmoving brothers, he felt as though rooted in the earth. He gazed out upon the silent countryside, and heard the distant train rumble into silence.

Ah! if only the beating of his heart could catch the rhythm of those tranquil constellations which never moved from their appointed course! But his true soul-sister, surely, was one of those shooting stars at which, as a child, he had gazed on mid-August nights. They fell so quickly, that, before he had had time to formulate a wish, they had vanished for ever into the sleeping stillness of the blue-black sky.

II

THE Château de Lur was one of those long, low-built houses of the Gironde which are known locally as "char-treuses". The late Marquis had added to it a slate-roofed construction in which to house his library, all that remained of a magnificent collection got together by an ancestor round about the year 1750. On the north side of the main building was a semicircular flight of steps, added in the reign of Louis XVI, where now wild mignonette flowered between the cracked stones. A row of limes, which had remained weakly because of the equinoctial gales, separated the house from an extensive slope of meadow-land. Beyond lay the landscape of Benauge, the "Entre Deux Mers", a swelling land of close-set uplands, streaked with vines planted in straight, ruled rows, broken here and there by isolated tufted elms which impressed themselves upon the eye by reason of their rarity. On the south side, two wings, one containing an orangery, the other a wine-store with the rooms inhabited by the Favereau family, enclosed a narrow courtyard which, even in winter, was so warm that mimose flourished in the open. Two low walls, each with a pillar formerly surmounted by rustic emblems, and linked by an archway covered with age-old ivy, separated this courtyard from the pleached alleys of hornbeam which were the glory of Lur. A wide central nave, and two lateral aisles, led to a long terrace overlooking the valley of the Garonne. At its western end stood an octagonal, half-ruined, gazebo. The parquet blocks, set in a pattern of concentric circles, were bulging. Damp had dislodged most of the panelling from the walls, and the whole place had become a store for disused rakes, spades and watering-pots. . . . Westwards stretched thick plantations of oaks, beeches and chestnuts, through which twisting and converging paths had been cunningly contrived. These plantations were the only concession permitted at Lur to the art of landscape gardening. Beyond them was a vast extent of luxuriant vineyards, their thick clusters of grapes and leaves sunning themselves in the blaze and torpor of July. On the far horizon rose the three crosses of the Viridis Calvary. . . . On the east, the many openings cut in the pleached alleys all faced the view. An orchard presented to the sun's rays its crowded clusters of ripe fruit. Now and again an apple would fall, spattering its contents on the hard ground.

Claude had been in the garden since six o'clock. His father had given him a day off for rest and relaxation. He intended to taste to the full the pleasure of each passing moment, and lay now, stretched at full length upon the heavy, clayey soil which it took four oxen, and then only with difficulty, to plough. He would, he decided, spend hours on the terrace, gazing at the

distant scene which had held for him, since childhood, an
inexhaustible charm, so endless were the variations brought to
it by weather and the changing seasons. Just where earth met
heaven he could glimpse the heathy country of Les Landes, a
motionless dark line of silence where, on calm evenings, could
be seen and heard the flash and rumble of the distant storms,
and the smoke of heath fires staining the overhanging sky with
yellow.

When siesta time came round, Claude, who had a key to
the library, opened the little door of the annexe which gave
on to the courtyard, and climbed the wooden stairs to the high-
ceilinged room with its four windows from which he could
look straight across to the horizon. The room had a faded
freshness, a smell of dust and mildew, but, more especially, of
old books. The silence there was absolute, the rather frightening
silence of rooms into which no one ever comes, rooms that
remain plunged in a half-light, and retain, even in the height
of summer, something of winter's icy moisture. He opened
the sash-windows and pushed back the heavy shutters. In a
flash the glare of afternoon filled this space which, for months,
had been hermetically sealed, indifferent to the changing
seasons, motionless in its cloistered darkness, with all its load
of philosophy and poetry. Here Claude had spent innumerable
summer days, and read until he was gorged with reading.
None but he had a fondness for this place of refuge. Its furnish-
ings were of the scantiest: a roughly-made table, a leather sofa
which had lost most of its stuffing, a set of steps for reaching
the topmost shelves – that was all. The Marquis de Lur had
never read anything but the catalogue of sporting equipment
issued by a gun-maker in Saint-Etienne. The new owners,
thought Claude, would be more likely to develop a taste for
his chosen hiding-place. What was there for a young man and
a young girl to do at Lur, apart from reading? He knew from

Monsieur Garros that Edward Dupont-Gunther was an amateur painter. He remembered that the two of them were Protestants. They would, he supposed, indulge frequently in "free-examination" and hunt endlessly through the pages of books for rules of conduct. Perhaps he would be shut out from this paradise, and that, after all, would perhaps be for the best. From now on his thoughts must be all of the soil. He must concern himself only with puzzling out the movements of the heavenly bodies, and reading the signs of weather in the sky. Nevertheless, just as the smoky kitchen at home had reminded him of his childhood, so now this cool, dusty sofa brought back the feelings of his adolescence, the dawning of that early period of maturity which was working in him still, those sad, yet blessed, hours when, with an uneasy conscience, he had knowingly been guilty of the sin of dabbling in wicked books. Memory came flooding back. . . . Outside it was August that lay in a blaze of heat upon the suffering vines, and the shrilling of the cicadas was but the monotonous plaint of growing things dying of thirst. Drunken bumble-bees were thumping against the ceiling: a burning ray of dazzling light forced its way through the closed shutters, quivering like an arrow that had come to rest in the thick target of the darkness. . . . He remembered one day in particular . . . what was the book he had been reading? – Ah, yes! the first volume of *Les Mémoires d'Outre-Tombe*. It had made him aware of his developing body. He could feel again all the urgency of his sixteen years. The same Sylph who had enchanted François-René de Chateaubriand had brought unease into the heart of the country lad lying protected from the dog-days in this cold, deserted library.

In a pierglass, standing low against the wall, he could see reflected a young man who was not so very different from the strapping boy who once, so long ago, had sat here, dreaming. He leaned his hot, flushed face against the glass, and the damp palms of his hands. Was it from the depths of the past, or from the days which lay ahead, that this ecstasy of melancholy was welling up and filling all his consciousness? Was it a last adieu to youth now dead and gone, or the burning breath which strikes the sailor in the face as the ship draws near an unknown coast? What was the nature of the threat he felt? He forced himself up from the sofa, and went down the inside staircase which led to the first floor of the Château. All along the vaulted corridor silent rooms stood waiting for, and dreading, the coming of their unknown masters. The pierglasses, the unfamiliar vases of a tender, muted colour, the smell of old chintzes, filled him with sensations that once had been familiar to persons now long dead. On the ground-floor the business of airing was proceeding in the drawing-room and dining-room which lay on either side of the hall where the billiard-table stood.

A girl was wielding a broom, while a full-bodied, dark-skinned lady was issuing conflicting orders in a deep contralto voice. Claude stopped short, somewhat taken aback, and the lady, choosing from among the trinkets dangling from her stomach, a tortoiseshell lorgnette, pointed it at him like a gun.

"What are you doing here, young man?"

"I am the bailiff's son ma'am . . . I am very sorry, ma'am . . . when the Marquis was still alive, I was in charge of the library . . . I just came along to see whether everything was all right."

"Oh, so you're the little seminarist, are you?"

Her smile revealed a mouth full of gold fillings. A blue vein showed prominently on her unhealthy-looking forehead, where the presence of two kiss-curls (they looked as though they had been painted there) showed how conscious she was of her Spanish appearance.

"I suppose you found life in that reverend establishment rather too austere, eh?"

With her three chins crushed against her bosom she looked the young man up and down. She appeared to be pleased by what she saw, for, crossing her hands behind her back and giving a jut to her bottom, she said, with a roguish air, and as though they had been old friends:

"I shouldn't say you are what one might call a cold type!"

Claude was amazed. This virago looked quite capable, as the saying goes, of gobbling him up.

"I expect you're wondering who I am? Let me introduce myself: I am Madame Gonzales, Mademoiselle Dupont-Gunther's companion. No doubt you find it surprising that a lady should be so humbly employed?"

Then, without wasting a moment, as though anxious that he should not remain in doubt of the social eminence of a Gonzales, she went on to explain that, although she was the daughter of a Spanish grandee, and the widow of an important Bayonne banker, she had found herself faced by the necessity of earning a living. Madame Gonzales was extremely fluent, expressing herself with a sort of languorous loquacity, like a naturally talkative person who for the last two days had had no one with whom to chatter. Her conversation showed the self-satisfaction of a "lady" whose obsessive mania it was to dazzle her listeners with an account of past splendours, and to arouse their sympathy by a detailed enumeration of her present reduced circumstances. She announced that she had been at once the happiest and most wretched of women: admitted that her husband had ruined himself that she might live like a princess, but left the young man in no doubt that after the disasters which had befallen her, she had astounded her relations by the ease with which she had managed to support herself and her daughter.

Claude thought to himself that he must be about as satisfactory a recipient of these confidences as one of the armchairs. He was careful not to display too great an interest in what he heard, nor too great a lack of it, but found a distinct pleasure in sniffing the effluvium given off by his companion, which was that of a full-fleshed woman who tended her person with some care.

"That," she wound up, "explains how it is that I have spent the last ten years under Monsieur Dupont-Gunther's roof. He has instructed me to make this old ruin habitable. He is not an easy man, but I can twist him round my little finger."

With an almost maternal gesture she patted the young man on the cheek, then, after assuring him that he would find a good friend in her, called to the housemaid and went with her up to the first floor.

Claude examined the drawing-room where almost nothing had been changed since the death of the Marquis. The ancient damask on the walls showed bright patches where the old family portraits had been taken down. A grand-piano had been installed some days before his arrival: perhaps in the evenings he would hear a little music through the trees. . . . He was aware of the stairs creaking under the weight of Madame Gonzales, and took to his heels only just in time. It was the hour at which cicadas make their way down the tree-trunks in the wake of the declining sun. He stopped in front of a vine-plant, lifted the leaves to which the sulphate had imparted a bluish colour, and looked to see whether there was any trace of blight on the clusters of green grapes. From a heap of burning leaves on one of the paths smoke was rising, as in some illustration to the Scriptures depicting the sacrifice of Abel. He went down the hill towards Viridis where flocks of screaming swallows and of pigeons were circling the Italianate campanile. The shops on the Square, which did a roaring trade in medals and rosaries on days of pilgrimage, were empty. In the church a last glow of fading daylight caught the garlands of little padded hearts, the gilded frame round a bridal wreath, a pair of epaulettes like those of the Duc d'Aumale, and a picture in which the bed of a sick man was draped with white curtains, and the Virgin was shown in a corner of the ceiling. He set himself mechanically to decipher the inscription, thereby keeping himself from being lulled to sleep by the drowsy drone of Vespers. "In 182 . . . Madame La Duchesse d'Angoulême visited Viridis with a numerous company for the purpose of placing the arms of her illustrious husband under the protection of Our Lady. . . ." He genuflected before the flame-encircled image of the Virgin, who was displayed in her ordinary, workaday clothes, for she, too, had a richly furnished wardrobe and changed her adornments on Sundays and Festivals. He stayed meditating at the feet of Her whose name was never absent from his lips when the angelus sent forth its summons at evening and at dawn. Ah! more than ever would he need Her help now that his only companion would be the warm, soft earth so closely in league with the flesh, from which on stormy evenings there rose a smell which seemed to be the very breath and fragrance of desire. . . . He prayed that the Virgin would protect him against his pagan brothers, the trees, against the arrogant splendour of the oaks, against the limes which smelt of love and passion. Might She bring to him a surer comfort than the blind, deaf constellations of the sky, with their names of evil gods!

He remembered the parish priest, the abbé Paulet, who was his friend, and felt surprised to think how pleased he had been when the housekeeper had told him that the Curé had gone on holiday and would be away for a month, pleased because that meant that he could yield to the mental sloth which made him unwilling to explain the movement of his heart, and to embark on the exercise of refuting vain objections. As he walked home, a large star was twinkling in the west, like a last remnant of the heat, and insects were vibrating in the darkness. A few country-folk called a good-night, and passed on without stopping because they failed to recognize him. He went early to his room, and, true to the promise he had made to Monsieur Garros, said his prayers. From all the villages of Benauge men could see his lamp shining upon this colloquy between a true child of the earth and God.

III

CLAUDE was awakened very early by the singing of birds in the pleached alleys: blackbirds and nightingales whom daylight does not silence: those, too, who nest in roofs and rafters: sparrows and swallows, these last so close that he could almost think them in the room with him, and, indeed, they sometimes did come in, marking the tiled floor with their white droppings. From his window he could look down on the wine-store, and note the tiles which his feet had broken when, as a small boy, he had roamed the roofs like a skinny cat. Away beyond, in the blue of dawn, he could see the dense mass of the hornbeams drenched in the light of the rising sun, rustling with the criss-cross flight of birds, and noisy with their drunken trilling. The moon had risen so late that her light was mingled with the day, and held its own against the climbing sun. The swaying tree-tops, caught in this unreal confusion of dawn and moonlight, set his mind dreaming of the world's first age.

A blaze of summer heat overflowed the horizon. The sun rose into the sky as though accomplishing a slow and leisurely victory. With tousled hair, and his bare feet stuck into rope-soled sandals, he went down the steep wooden staircase leading to the kitchen. His father was already there, sitting in front of a half-empty litre. The wine which the bottle no longer contained showed in his face. He rose from his chair to give Claude a morning kiss of salutation, and the young man noticed that his father had breakfasted off a crust of bread plentifully rubbed with garlic. The fresh morning breeze was bellying the curtain which hung before the door.

"There's work for you, young fellow. The boss has told me to dig up the vine plants on that bit of ground near the alley, as he wants to make a tennis-court or some such. 'Twouldn't be so bad if they was old 'uns, but the old master had grafted'm some ten years gone. Still, orders is orders. The big lady up at the Château says she's expecting them all here to-day. Off with you, lad. The ground's ready cleared, and there's naught for you to do 'cept to bring up some soil from the road and run the roller over it."

Claude accepted the offer of a good swig before setting off. Then, in the yard, under the pomegranates with their scarlet blooms which brought to mind the lips of the cigar-makers, he set the handle of the pump creaking. The lip of the pot-bellied well-head was marked with a groove made by a chain in the old days when water had been brought up in a pail. He took off his shirt. The water gushed from a rusty pipe over his hair and into his ears. He filled the hollow trough, and, bending down, saw his face reflected. Fourtille, with a bucket in each hand, joined him. She reminded him of a picture of an Athenian girl which he had once seen in the Manual of Greek History written by the abbé Gagnol for use in Christian schools. He was revolted by her thick neck, her man's hands, and the stupid glitter in her small, round, hen-like eyes. It made him uneasy, too, to think that every morning she would be on the look-out for him at the pump. She was trying with a sort of heavy-handed slyness to establish a secret understanding between them. This morning she was complaining because the pump was too near the Great House and when the new owners arrived there wouldn't be much chance to talk.

"But you can allus help I with the pails." Claude had been foolish enough to render her this service once already, and knew only too well what it might lead to. To reach the cowman's dwelling from the yard meant going through the dark wine-store, and he did not like the idea. On this particular morning, he missed the door and stumbled. With calculated clumsiness Fourtille came to his assistance.

Without mincing his words he told her that he had got work to do, and couldn't hang about there with her. He went off whistling, with his hands in his pockets. He rounded the corner of the alley where patches of sunlight were lying on the ground. This was the piece of land where there should have been flourishing vines: but an unknown young man and an unknown young woman were going to use it for knocking balls at each other. There was not a scrap of shade. The sun beat fiercely down upon the back of his neck while he filled the wheel-barrow, which Pascal had routed out, with earth. At vine-level peach and plum trees cast quite inadequate blobs of shadow. He could hear Abel's drawling voice urging on the two oxen, one of which, by long tradition, was always called Caubet, the other, Lauret. Heat had settled down for the day. Over towards Benauge he could see it vibrating over the empty roads. Away in the plain the Garonne was glittering like a fish among the rushes. He could not see the meadows, but soft, white butterflies had drifted in from them and were aimlessly pursuing one another among the vines with their strong smell of growing things. The postman, bent double like a soul in torment over his handlebars, tossed two letters to the young man without stopping. On one of the envelopes Claude recognised the neat, sloping hand of Monsieur Garros to which in the old days he had grown accustomed from seeing the rather tactless scribblings in the margins of his essays. He tore open the second without the slightest feeling of impatience. The four pages, each as regular as a passage of print, in which Monsieur de Floirac hoped to enlist his enthusiasm for Monsieur Leroy's theories about symbolism and dogma, he read through without pleasure. He had too much to distract him from such abstract words: the noisy chattering of black-birds in the bushes, and the thudding of his own blood. Fourtille passed by, lower down the slope, with a spade on her shoulder. Her buttocks moved as she walked, and her loins, which were tightly confined by a dark blue apron.

Overcome by lassitude, he sat down on his barrow, thinking of the stew and the white wine to come, and, after them, a siesta in the deep country silence where Pan was dozing. Below him, on the road, he saw a moving cloud of dust, heard the sound of a horn, and realized that a motor-car was coming towards the house. It glided up the hill without the slightest sign of effort, and he followed it with his eyes as he would have done any country cart. Now and then the trees hid it from his view, but its throbbing drew nearer. It must be making for the main gate. . . . It passed through. . . . Here, no doubt, were the strangers, the young masters. Claude's heart continued to beat as regularly as before. If this was the master, he had better be getting back to his work. At eleven o'clock, he returned to the courtyard where the sunlight smelled of the dark, swelling heliotrope round which the bees were humming. For the second time that morning he went and washed at the well. It was then that, from behind the half-closed shutters of the ground floor he heard a nasal voice saying:

"I shall have that well filled in." For the first time he realized that, from then on, an unknown power would be in control at Lur.

When he reached home, he found Favereau, Maria, Abel and Fourtille sitting with their food untouched before them. Favereau, whom Monsieur Gunther had been nagging among the vines, was airing his views:

"Doesn't know a thing about vines, and thinks he can tell *me* what to do. . . ."

"Yes," said Abel. "And he thinks the paths is too wide, and we're wasting ground. Says he'll plant three where there's nobut two now. I told un as in dry weather when the ground's hard two oxen's not more than enough to work the plough, and that we got to leave 'nough space atween the rows. You should a seen how he took that!"

Favereau turned his bloodshot eyes on Maria.

"Hey! old lazy bones, aren't we going to have anything to eat?"

She got up, and soon the white dishes were gleaming on the table. Claude, a loaf pressed to his chest, was leaning over the soup-tureen, cutting bread. Those round the table worked their jaws slowly, saying nothing. First one hen, then two, cautious and greedy, hesitated, and grew bold. Claude ate scarcely at all, but drank a great deal, laying his hands, now and again, against the sides of the oozing water-jug. His mother, who had scarcely any teeth, was mumbling her food, like a ruminant animal, while her eyes wandered over the yellowing photographs on the wall, in which the faces of those two brothers whom Claude had never known were growing dimmer with the passing years. Dinner done, he escaped into the north-side meadow which sloped down

towards Benauge – the best place for a siesta. It was very close
to the Great House, but he expected that none of the Dupont-
Gunther family would stick their noses out of doors at this
time of the day. Through his lowered lids the noon blaze
struck fiercely on his eyes, filling his own particular darkness
with whirling, spreading suns. One single cicada was shrilling
away with a monotonous intensity, as though to give the
measure of the afternoon silence in this daze of country
summer.

Suddenly, a strange music burst through the half-closed
shutters, and spread in a tumult of sound through the glare.
Claude sat up, and, with his head leaning against a lime-tree
trunk, listened. Memory brought back to him the large, white-
washed common-room of the seminary where there had been
an ancient piano and a wheezy harmonium. It was there that
he had learned to love, in addition to plainsong, Bach, César-
Franck . . . but they had not prepared him for these wild
sounds.

The door was pushed open, and Madame Gonzales appeared
wearing a white linen dress which was so tight that she was
obviously finding it difficult to get down the steps. Claude
judged that it was too late to run away, and stayed where he
was, amazed that so large a body and such seemingly vigorous
legs could be supported on such tiny feet and teetering heels.
The music stopped, and he could hear the sound of a piano
being shut. Madame Gonzales walked in his direction. Seeing
a human figure half upright in the grass, she waxed indignant.

"This comes of having the servants' quarters so close to the
house – always some country lout hanging round!"

Claude got up with an awkward gesture of apology. At
sight of him, the lady melted into a softer mood.

"Oh! it's you, is it – the baby priest? All I meant was that one
is always falling over one or other of the estate people. . . . I

don't understand how anyone can endure having peasants and live-stock at their door. The very food tastes of manure! . . . When I complained of the flies in the gravy, Monsieur Dupont explained that it was because of the oxen which we could hear rattling their chains in the feeding-troughs."

Claude, anxious to be gone, tried to make his escape with a vague expression of agreement. But the lady motioned him to stay where he was.

"That man won't so much as consider having alterations made. He is quite incapable of shouldering any expense that won't bring in a return. When Monsieur Gonzales bought a property, he always had everything pulled down and rebuilt in accordance with his own ideas – or, rather, with mine. Anyone as sensitive as you are will understand me when I say that it is hard to have to live with Baeotians!"

Claude said stupidly: "Oh, no ma'am, no!"

"Mean as you make 'em, and hate Art!"

"But . . . isn't Monsieur Edward a painter? Besides, I heard him just now playing the piano."

"It was the music that sent me skedaddling, my dear boy! I do claim to know something about music: after all, I *did* get an honourable mention at the Bordeaux Conservatoire. Not that I was ever a professional, but my father always insisted on my having the best masters. These composers Madamoiselle May pretends to think so highly of – just noise, dear boy, just noise! Those animals in there say they like it – pure snobbery, that's all it is, and done to annoy me! But one has got to keep on the right side of the Lord and Master – the sooner you realize that, the better!" Her face wrinkled into a sly smile. She looked like a superannuated actress playing Carmen in a provincial theatre.

"I must ask you to forgive me, ma'am: I have to roll the tennis court."

Madame Gonzales went on without listening to him.

"Music? Just you wait till you've heard my daughter Edith, who'll be joining me here in August. When *she* plays, what brilliance, what brio! – very different from all this discordant din!"

She seemed suddenly to realize how familiarly she was talking to a "peasant", pinched her lips, distended her bust, and said, in a haughty voice:

"To work, young man, to work! You're wasting your time here!"

She returned to the house, and Claude, harnessing himself to the roller, began to move it backwards and forwards over the tennis-court. He was conscious of a sort of animal pleasure. No matter how much energy he put into the task, he could not exhaust himself. The heat, far from overwhelming him, bore him up like water.

"But the earth isn't packed tight! The balls'll never bounce on it!"

He raised his streaming face. A young man and a young woman were looking down at him from the terrace. Monsieur Edward was wearing white flannels. The low collar of his soft shirt made his neck look longer than it really was. The wide cuff revealed a wrist encircled by a platinum bracelet. At first Claude could not take his eyes from this strange adornment. Thick hair, brushed back and plastered down, grew high on the young man's forehead. His face was highly coloured, and had a look almost of red gold. Between his lips was a long cigarette-holder which filled the afternoon with a smell of rich, city streets. May was holding her sun-hat by the strings. Claude could see nothing of her but a pair of cold grey eyes which did not so much avoid his own as move hither and thither as though nervously unable to come to rest. . . . Monsieur Edward said, with a bored air:

"It's no use rolling unless you put down earth from the road first: that's a tomfool way of doing things!"

May dug a hole in the court with her heel. Edward went on: "Take that barrow and a shovel and fetch some earth. This court's got to be playable tomorrow!"

Claude was already preparing to obey when Favereau appeared. Siesta had sent the blood to his face. His trousers were hanging down so far that it was a wonder they kept up at all.

"Where 'you off to, Claude?" The young man moved away with his father, and heard Edward give vent to an exclamation: "I say, we *have* put our foot in it – that's the little priest!"

In the evening, Claude from his window watched a storm blowing up. The trees all started rustling at once. A wind from the south was tearing great furrows in their massed foliage so that it looked like an angry sea. A shutter banged. But, dominating the noise of the wind in the branches, and the unceasing vibration of insects, the music which had disturbed his siesta was now filling the darkness, mingling with it like the voice of an unseen ocean. Then the piano ceased, the wind dropped. "The storm isn't coming our way, after all," murmured Claude. The rain was falling on the leaves which the breeze had ceased to trouble: the smell of the earth penetrated the night air as though it were some obscure upward gush of vegetable ecstasy. Claude's body seemed to be softened and flooded by the rain, and he was conscious of that delicious exhaustion which follows on the heels of hard physical work. Half-naked on the bed, which he had not troubled to turn down, he lay, lulled to sleep by the hiss and rustle of the countryside.

IV

NEXT morning there was no sunrise. Favereau, with his white wine in front of him, was saying all the things he kept religiously for rainy weather.

"Vines, they like heat. It's rain that brings the blight: the more you spray 'em with sulphate, the more the water washes it away."

There was a smell in the kitchen of fat, bran-mash, and country bodies whose only bath is the sun. Claude was reading *Graziella*. All of a sudden, Favereau sprang to attention. Monsieur Edward had entered the room, looking rather shy. He shook hands with everybody, withdrawing his own a little too quickly, and asked the lad to be so good as to have a word with him in the barn.

"When I spoke to you yesterday, down on the tennis-court, I did not know who you were. It's not for me to give orders to the son of our bailiff . . . to. . . ." (he hesitated, trying to find the right word) ". . . to a talented young man like you. . . ."

Claude replied that it was the most natural thing in the world for him to take orders. They stood facing one another like two small boys who have just been introduced and told to run away and play. Edward was the first to recover his self-assurance, and remarked – as he might have done in a drawing-room to a lady who had no gift of conversation – that this rain was just about as beastly as it could be. Claude politely expressed the hope that it would not cause him to think too badly of Lur. He kept his eyes down, and Edward noticed that though he had the body of a young giant, and was burned black by the sun, his face was markedly intelligent. He reflected that it might well be worth the trouble to try and bring this young country chap out. Meanwhile, Claude was feeling no little surprise that this scion of the bourgeoisie, his master and his elder, should have shown so much delicacy.

"I envy you for being able to enjoy that sort of stuff still" – said Edward, pointing to *Graziella*: "I notice," he added, "that it's the 1852 edition."

Claude, delighted to find that his new master had some knowledge of books, replied that he had come to love Lamartine as a result of reading him. He felt himself blushing when Edward mentioned his favourite authors, none of whose names did he know. He received an assurance that he could have free access to the library, just as in the old days. All round them the drain-gutters were overflowing, and the water was cutting channels in the paths. The swallows were skimming low, and concealing themselves in the rafters, which were loud with the cheeping of birds.

The dinner bell had to be rung three times before Edward took any notice of it. Claude, seated at his own meal, let his father drone on without interruption. He was thinking that Edward was just like the young men of whom he had caught a glimpse when he had visited the home of his friend, de Floirac. Their life was something he would never know, and he tried to imagine it, peopling the scene he conjured up with active young men in soft shirts, shooting parties, early morning meets, riders, scarcely more than boys, in yellow leather gaiters, dogs barking round the big shooting-brakes, and a general air of excitement and happy anticipation in the fresh, clean air which is the aftermath of fine nights when the countryside awakens from its sleep.

After lunch, since the rain showed no sign of lifting, he went back to the barn, and standing there with the swish of falling

water all about him, said to himself: 'It was just here that we
were chatting a while back.' He heard the quick footsteps of
somebody hurrying through the rain. He dared not hope that
it was Edward, but, a moment later, saw that young man
appear. He was running, his bare head thrown back. He told
Claude, breaking off frequently to get his breath, that he and
his sister had thought it might be a good way of killing time
to rearrange the library, and that they needed his help.

By way of the outside staircase they climbed to the big
room where on the previous evening, Claude had brooded over
thoughts of himself at sixteen. The first thing he saw was the
young girl, May, leaning in the embrasure of one of the
windows, Behind her a heavy ceiling of cloud was showing
patches of metallic blue through tattered rents. The rain had
stopped, but a wind was making the trees shake and drip.
The birds were twittering in that peculiar way they have after
a storm. Claude was afraid that she might follow her brother's
example, and start apologizing. But she merely held out her
hand. Edward was talking about some of the interesting
editions he had seen. Claude, not listening to him, looked at his
own reflection in the pier-glass where, yesterday, he had seen
the dreamy, solemn schoolboy he once had been. To-day the
glass showed him – for the first time, it seemed to him – a mass
of rather too curly hair, a made-up red tie, and a pair
of enormous hands with dirty nails, and a shirt of grey
flannel.

While, just for form's sake, he asked Edward whether he
proposed to arrange the books alphabetically by authors, he was
conscious only of one desire – to disappear. May, who, so far,
had said nothing, began to explain in a rather breathless,
hurried voice, like that of shy people anxious to relapse into
silence, that in her brother's Paris rooms the books were
arranged according to the colour of their bindings. The mass

of hair gathered into her neck, seemed to drag her rather too small head backwards. Only now and again could Claude catch a glimpse of the ice-blue eyes which, for most of the time, were veiled by slightly reddened lids. At a loss for something to say, he asked, rather foolishly, whether she was fond of reading.

"Me?, fond of reading? I can get on with a very few books. Madame Gonzales, who has a Library subscription, is always girding at me for not keeping abreast with the new ones."

"What are the very few books?" asked Claude, suddenly interested, and unskilled in tact.

She drew her brows together in a frown, said, rather mincingly, that it really didn't matter, and sauntered slowly across to the shelves.

Claude had been quite unaware of the snub, but Edward, fearing that he might feel hurt, revealed the fact that his sister's private collection was confined to the Bible, Aeschylus, and, among the moderns, only Baudelaire.

"Don't let yourself be dazzled," said May: "I scarcely ever open any of them except the Bible."

Edward went on: "Music's the only thing she really cares about."

Claude, now completely at his ease, remarked rather pompously that he·had been awakened by "floods of harmony", that he, too, loved music passionately, though apart from a few Gregorian chants and pieces for the organ, he was appallingly ignorant. Edward, squatting on the sofa, lit a cigarette which smelled of ambergris, incense, and dried rose-petals. With a great show of choosing his words very carefully, he began to say things which Claude had long treasured in his heart. He said that for those who could not remain contented with appearances, music tore away the veils, compelled them to look death in the face, and that this confrontation produced an intense species of pleasure. He explained that in the case of certain young friends of his who had killed themselves, music had provided the last bond that kept them attached to life. He mentioned one of them by name, who had spent the last few days of his life lying on the drawing-room floor, refusing to let his sister leave the piano, and saying "more! more!"

Claude, who had by now entirely forgotten his earlier wish to escape, was staring intently at Edward's lips, like a child listening to a story. Now and again he ventured a sidelong glance at May who, seated close to her brother, had her arms raised and her hands clasped behind her head. He remembered, later, how he had replied that music could also be prayer, a cry of joy and love, an act of faith, and how Edward had agreed, mentioning Beethoven and the Ninth Symphony. "But in Paris," he said, "people are beginning to react against all music that has too ponderous a content, music to which one can listen only with one's head in one's hands. What they want now is something stripped, simple and spare."

The rain had begun once more to isolate them within a fine web shot through with occasional fleeting gleams of sun. In the middle of the high room, fragrant with the smell of old bindings and tobacco, Claude felt as though he were outside time, as though this moment must surely be eternal. He said that in this choice he had made to return to his true origins, what he would most miss would be music. He told them that once, and only once, when he was staying with the parents of his friend Floirac, he had heard a woman singing, and that the sound of her voice was with him still.

"What a pity" said Edward, "that May will never sing for anybody except me. . . . To hear her would be a revelation for you."

To this remark May added, somewhat sharply: "I have a

horror of being made use of to help people digest their dinners, or to fill up the time till their cars are announced. I'd rather die than be an addition to the meal, like coffee and liqueurs. But I will sing for you, if it would give you the slightest pleasure. . . ."

Claude, speechless with embarrassment, could only make a gesture. With feverish haste, and a strange, disproportionate air of happiness, Edward dragged them off to the drawing-room. May took her seat at the piano while he looked out a song for her.

To Claude it seemed that the rain drops on the leaves, the wind in the limes, and the whole drowned countryside, had paused to listen, or, rather, that the sounds of the dripping afternoon had passed into the young girl's voice. The piece chosen by Edward was called l'Invitation au Voyage. Each phrase struck against his heart like a tiny wave. He seemed to glimpse inaccessible joys, a rending happiness.

The door opened. May shut the piano, and rose to her feet. Claude saw a fat, stocky man. His close-cropped hair was almost white and threw his purple cheeks into horrible relief. He looked like a picture of sudden death.

"What are you doing here, young man?" He fixed on Claude a blue-green glare, in which the youth, in spite of his embarrassment, could not help recognizing the colour of May's eyes. Monsieur Dupont-Gunther was wearing a covert-coat. On his little finger was a ring set with a single diamond. An excessively heavy chain lay like a bar across his stomach. Claude's voice stuck in his throat. It was Edward who answered the question, with a nonchalant air.

"I asked Claude Favereau to help us arrange the library."

"This is not the library." Anger had caused a vein to swell in Monsieur Dupont-Gunther's forehead. His hands, which he had clasped behind his back, were trembling.

"No one here has a right to make use of my people!"
Then, turning to Claude: "You'll take your orders from me,
young man, and from nobody else! I give you fair warning.
Now go and tell Favereau that I want to see him at the wine-
store."

When Claude had left the room, Monsieur Dupont-Gunther
turned his squat body to face Edward. He looked like a bull-
dog ready to pounce. Edward said to his sister: "My dear, better
go to your room. . . ." She obeyed, holding herself very
upright, and not deigning to give her father so much as a
look.

"You dare! . . . you dare! . . ." he spluttered. Edward,
leaning against the piano, his hands in his pockets, his large,
red-lipped mouth distended in a deliberate smile, his head
thrown back, faced with complete calm the gross and furious
little man.

"You are perfectly right, father, and I realize that I was at
fault. I should have known better than to bring this young
man here. Please accept my apologies."

"Y . . . you think you can get out of it as easily as that, do
you?"

"I can scarcely believe that you intend to give me a beating,
or to put me on a diet of dry bread. Good-bye: what you need,
I think, is to be left to yourself."

He sketched a bow with his head, moved away with the
gliding gait which was peculiar to him, and opened the door
so quietly that he very nearly collided with Madame
Gonzales who was listening outside."

"I was on the point of coming in," she stammered.

Edward apologized with calculated insolence for having
disturbed her habitual methods of procedure, and withdrew.

Madame Gonzales came to a halt in front of the master of
the house. He was still standing where his son had left him, his

legs straddled, and the stupid look of a man listening to the pounding of his own blood. She smiled at him in the pleasantest possible way, with her hands in the pockets of her apron, and in a high-pitched, rather sing-song voice, said:

"Don't you think it would be rather a good thing if you put your feet in a mustard bath?"

It was a most unfortunate remark. To an accompaniment of growls and snarls, Bertie Dupont-Gunther shouted that he wasn't yet in his second childhood, that he was sick of being ridden over rough-shod in his own house, that he'd make a clean sweep of the lot of them, that he'd had enough of always seeing her old bitch's. . . .

She trembled under the shock of the word he had flung at her, bridled, drew herself up on her high heels, and murmured that she was a poor, weak women, and that there was only one thing for her to do. He was a past master in the art of assuming that air of excessive politeness by which hot-tempered men, when they have lost control of themselves, recover their authority, and turn loss into gain. Though he was far coarser, far more headstrong, than any of his estate workers, Bertie always played at being the gentleman.

"You must forgive me, Mélanie. You caught me at a bad moment. You mustn't, I beg of you, ever doubt the warmth of my feelings for you."

His too short upper lip, with its stubbly pepper-and-salt moustache, lifted for a moment and revealed a rodent's tooth. Madame Gonzales, in the course of a long and eventful life, had never acquired that deep knowledge of the male which she might have been supposed to possess. She believed that this sudden change of tone heralded a return of tenderness in one over whom she quite rightly assumed that she had no small influence, though for many years now Bertie had given up asking of her what she would have been only too happy not to refuse. He had installed her in his house on the pretext of having somebody to teach his children music. This he had done during the life-time of the late Madame Dupont-Gunther, that proud, unhappy lady, whom Mélanie had never tired of wounding, humiliating and gloating over. Though old now, and grotesque, she still clung tenaciously to her position. Once past fifty, however, Monsieur-Gunther had increasingly turned from such mature charms as she had to offer. Consequently, he was not within measurable distance of grasping the significance of the tumultuous rise and fall of the lady's opulent bosom.

"Oh Bertie, Bertie, no matter what you may say, I could never doubt that! The bond between us is too strong ever to be broken!"

At this point she managed to burst into sobs.

"*That* sort of thing is all over and done with, my dear. Ancient history is ancient history. D'you mind if I light a cigar?"

She continued to dab her eyes just long enough to give herself time in which to realize the extent of her blunder: then, once again assuming the role of an almost maternal confidante, she made Bertie sit beside her on the sofa.

"What is it, dear friend, that has upset you? Do you find Edward's presence in this house unpleasing?"

Bertie growled:

"*That* conceited young puppy, *that* miserable dauber! – Since the children came into their mother's money, I've had no hold over them, no control."

Madame Gonzales expressed the opinion that the law in such matters was quite abominable.

"Well, it's no use crying over spilt milk," said Bertie. "Edward has already insisted on having undisputed say where his capital's concerned. I still have authority over May, but she'll soon be of age now."

"It's a very serious situation, Bertie. . . ."

"More serious than you think, my dear, but the key to the whole business is in your hands. Just you listen to me. May detests you."

"Dear child! Nothing will ever make me leave off returning good for evil. . . ."

"May detests you," went on Gunther, "and the success of my plan depends upon you becoming quite literally insupportable to her."

The lady protested that that would be very difficult, but Bertie replied, without mincing his words, that all she had to do was to be perfectly natural. She bridled at this, and pretended not to see why it should be necessary for her to become an object of hatred.

"Now, look here, my dear: if May's money is to remain in the family, she's got to marry young Castagnède, whose father, while he still lived, was my business associate. Old mother Castagnède takes great pride in the thought of the two families being connected: there's nothing she wants more, in spite of the difference of religion. But May's only got to get wind of my intentions to refuse point blank."

Madame Gonzales had to agree that the girl frequently laughed at the young man, "who's worth two of her".

"He's a perfect nit-wit," said Monsieur Dupont-Gunther, "and so much the better. As soon as you've driven my daughter to such a state of exasperation that she can't stand the sight of anybody in this house, Marcel Castagnède will providentially turn up. You won't be a loser, Mélanie. Incidentally I am delighted by this idea of yours of bringing your daughter here, the charming Edith, whom I haven't seen since she was in short frocks. The children'll be mad!"

The sharp rodent's teeth appeared again for a moment under the drawn-back lip.

Madame Gonzales looked at him, sighed, smiled:

"No one could see Edith without loving her, not even the jealous May."

"You'd better keep a sharp eye on me, then!" Monsieur Dupont-Gunther permitted himself to say, and proceeded to lay upon the lady the duty of "spying on the children" when he had gone back to Bordeaux, not to return until the following Sunday: she must listen to their every word, watch their every movement. All of a twitter, and swaying her hips as in the days when she was a young person with firm and succulent curves, Mélanie withdrew to her room, there to meditate in front of her daughter's photograph.

The main piece of furniture was an old painted bedstead hung with *toile de Jouy*. All about the room were scattered pots of make-up and sticks of rouge and monstrous cardboard hatboxes. The prevailing smell was of slops. All these things combined to proclaim the type of woman who was thus bringing shame on the old age of this ancient house. A last ray of sunshine played upon the synthetic glitter of her hair, and turned to gold the innumerable motes of rice-powder dancing in its path. With love and pride she looked at the photograph which was her surest weapon, her trump card.

At this same hour of the day, Edward and May were having tea in the young man's room. They had closed the shutters. A brass table-lamp cast a narrow circle of light. Its presence had brought their chairs into close proximity, and everything was conducive to intimate talk. Over the lyre-shaped mahogany sofa Edward had thrown a black and gold Persian shawl. In a vase of Decoeur pottery, which had the blue colour of a pebble washed smooth by a mountain torrent, stood a single rose. On the wall he had hung an Eugène Lamy water-colour from the Salon of 1840, showing a young girl seated at a piano, heavily upholstered chairs, and ladies half lost in voluminous skirts.

A Lucien de Rubempré was leaning against the mantel-piece.

"It really is very wrong of you, Edward, to make so much fuss of this young man. I know your little ways. I have so often seen you dazzling your friends of the moment, usually young women, and then leaving them high and dry and disillusioned. But in this case it's far worse."

Edward threw away his cigarette, opened the window, and pushed the shutters wide. The leaves were still dripping, and frogs were quietly croaking in the grass.

"That's most unfair of you, darling. This Claude inspires me with a far greater liking than any of those you say I have dropped in the past, people, all of them, who had lost the power to keep the same faces I had seen when I first set eyes on them. You are temperamentally too like me" (he smiled: the word had become a sort of cliché between them) "not to appreciate so sensitive a mind in so uncouth a body. He is a stranger to all we most hate – pose, affectation, all the artificialities which exasperate me beyond bearing, in myself and in others, but mostly in myself, in *us*. Come, be honest! Weren't you, too, rather fascinated? You sang for him, which is something you never do for anybody."

May smiled but said nothing. They could hear the purring of the car which was carrying Monsieur Gunther back to his labours and his mistresses. Close at hand the great bell rang for dinner in a rustle of Virginia creeper and jasmin. At table, Madame Gonzales ate with her elbows pressed to her side, and raised her glass with the little finger extended. She knew, that one should never show what one has in one's mouth, and her hermetically sealed lips compelled her to masticate her food at great length. As dinner drew to a close her cheeks became heavily flushed, and she turned away to dab at them with a leaf of *papier poudre*. The young people went into the drawing-room. Madame Gonzales did not follow them. But they knew that she was lurking somewhere in the shadows of the hall, with her ears pricked, for all her pretence of being sleepy.

Edward said something in a low voice to May, opened the piano, and chose a piece of music. In a voice that was scarcely more than a whisper, his sister said:

"Is it wide enough for him to hear?"

That night, Claude ate his own meal in silence. On the opposite side of the table his father was busily engaged in spreading small pieces of bacon on square hunks of bread. The big, bulky man emptied his glass at a gulp, and wiped his moustache with the back of his hand. Maria kept on getting up to bring in more food. Claude begged her to sit down. She said she had never had a meal in peace yet except in other people's houses, at weddings or funerals. The young man went up to his room and stood by the open window. The sound of footsteps on the Viridis road told him that the wind was from the east. At last the singing for which he had been waiting reached his ears, for he *had* been waiting, though he had not dared admit it to himself, waiting for that cry of entreaty, of nostalgic desire, of ardour and despair. In spite of the distance he could distinctly make out two lines of the song which recurred again and again. He kept on repeating them long after the meloncholy music had ceased. That he might murmur them once more before he slept, he neglected to say his prayers.

V

SIESTA. Claude could see men dotted about the pasture like the debris of a defeated army. They sprawled round the ricks with outflung arms, and handkerchiefs over their faces. For his part, he had no wish to sleep. He wanted to surrender himself, soul and body, to the heat which burned his life up in a greater Life. He dreamed that his feet had taken root, that his spread hands were twisted into branchy knots, that his head, responsive to a mounting sap, was swaying a great mop of dark leaves among the clouds. His father had told him to rake the paths. He picked up the golden stub of one of Edward's cigarettes, and stood for a long time staring at the trace of a small foot in the dried clay of the terrace. He felt a longing to go over to the chestnuts where, that morning, he had slung two hammocks. He wandered about within sight of them, and, from a distance, envied the motionless foliage which spread a world of silence above the sleeping forms of its young masters. A cicada awakened into sudden life, scraped unevenly for a while, then fell into its habitual rhythm and beat like the suffering heart of the brooding Cybele. In spite of himself he moved closer.

"Is that you, Claude?"

He ran forward. Edward was sitting on one of the hammocks, his hair tousled, his collar unbuttoned. May was lying at full length, modestly swathed to the ankles in her white dress, and the country lad was taken with wonder at the sight of two silver slippers weighing down the netted fabric of her airy bed, and looking like tiny fish. He was surprised when the girl turned on him a pair of smiling eyes, and held out her rather powerful hand, which her brother described as a pianist's. Edward gazed out across the plain which lay shimmering in the heat.

"What's that glittering down there?"

Claude burst into a guffaw of laughter:

"Why, that's the Garonne, Mister Edward!"

"How close it looks. I say, Claude, d'you know anywhere good for bathing?"

Claude replied that when he was a child he used to go to a spot between Saint-Pierre-d'Aurillac and Saint-Macaire, where there was a stretch of level sand under the willows: but it meant three-quarters-of-an-hour's walking to get there, and the same to come back, so that he had always got hot again and so lost the benefit of the cool water.

"We'll take the car," said Edward. The prospect of pleasure to come revived him. He gave a violent shaking to the hammock from which his sister had not stirred, and sent her scurrying to the dining-room to prepare a snack for them to take with them. Such feverish excitement made Claude feel uncomfortable, so out of all proportion did it seem to a simple bathing trip. He much preferred his young master in one of his gloomy and exhausted moods than a prey to this somewhat hysterical gaiety.

Edward took the wheel, with Claude beside him. May was alone on the back seat. The car slid smoothly forward. In the windscreen he could see May reflected, and kept his eyes fixed on that inaccessible image which quivered to the rhythm of the engine. The car slowly nosed its way down a lane leading to the river. While May got the picnic ready, the two young men plunged into a clump of willows. The river moved here so lazily that, at first, it was impossible to make out in which direction it was flowing. They undressed, and, after a few plunges, lay, floating, gazing upwards at the slumbering blue, abandoning themselves to the river's life, which seemed the very pulse of the living earth. Oh! exquisite contentment. Only the languid flight of a bird broke the calm radiance of the blue immensity. The sun shone level now and forced them to see the world through half-closed eyelids. Their slim bodies were caught between air and water. A fish leaped like a fleck of mercury. At last, torn from the water's warm embrace, the young men, filled with the pride of their physical well-being, puffed out their chests full in the sun's eye, and flexed the muscles of their arms on which no drop of moisture could now be seen.

May presided over their meal, bustling about, suddenly a little girl again, laughing as little girls always laugh.

"Hurry up! if you don't, all the greengages will be gone!"

They lay down upon the grass which bore them up as, only a short while before, the stream had done. Edward expressed astonishment that the "beauties of nature" served equally well as an argument for those who wished to see the Universe as the work of a creative intelligence, and those who believed only in matter and the operation of blind laws. Claude, as usual, put a blunt question which had an air of artlessness:

"And what is your view?"

Edward said that what he was most conscious of was a feeling of absence. All the theologian in Claude, all the intelligence trained since schoolboy days in controversy, took fire at that word "feeling". He even went so far as to allude to his employers' heresy. He remembered an excellent course of lectures given by Monsieur Garros who, having lived in Lot-et-Garonne where Protestants are thick on the ground, had been in a position to study at first hand the so-called Reformed Religion.

"You people can only "feel" either a presence or an absence. Your clergymen – deprived of the Sacraments, and of the one essential Sacrament – try, by means of endless sermons, which they do their best to make white-hot, to induce in their flock a succession of states of feeling."

Edward was amused to note the sudden swing-back to metaphysics in this young and uncouth creature. A little while before, lying in the river, he had been a complete animal: then, leaning stark naked against a willow, someone who had looked like the shepherd David. Now he was sitting with his shirt unfastened, revealing a sun-burned chest. May was eyeing the disputants uneasily. Edward took up the challenge.

"Doesn't your own Pascal say that God is known in the heart, and not the brain?"

Red-faced, bristling, and looking now like the seminarist who, not so long ago, had paced the school-yard with Monsieur de Floirac, Claude gave blow for blow, Yes, he said, God was known as the result of a movement of the soul, in a word, by love. Grace sets its seal upon the Christian. But once that inner knowledge is acquired, the faithful find outside themselves the source and origin of love. Someone exists, and that Someone is distinct from the creature, who knows where to find Him, and can eat of His flesh and drink of His blood.

Edward was still smiling. He was so utterly indifferent to the point at issue, that he made no attempt to pursue the argument. May, on the other hand, put a question:

"If you were trying to convert me, Claude, how would you go about it?"

"I would first ask whether you were not conscious of something lacking in your Church. You Protestants stand face to face with God, but from you to Him there is no direct road of access. Sermons and community prayers may be emotionally stirring, and can certainly give you the sensation of His presence, but except in those moments of collective fervour, He remains inaccessible."

At these words May, like all women at grips with abstract formulae, hesitated.

"It may be true that our weakness lies in our never knowing for certain whether we have proof: all the same, I quite honestly believe that your dogmas are childish, and the whole business of Catholicism just idolatry pure and simple."

Claude's back was up, and he forgot the deference due to Monsieur Dupont-Gunther's daughter.

"You are talking of things you know nothing about!"

The seminarist's contempt for this piece of female reasoning sounded only too obviously in his voice. But the girl seemed not to be aware of it. As though speaking to herself, she said:

"If I were a Catholic, I should love a rule of belief which has nothing to do with what I may feel or not feel: with the sense of tranquility which must come of believing what one is told to believe: but what would most satisfy me would be the certainty of divine forgiveness."

Claude clasped his hands: an exclamation was forced from him:

"Oh! Mademoiselle, what faults can *you* ever have committed?"

Edward burst out laughing. He felt uneasy, and, at the same time curious to hear what answer his haughty sister would make. She, however, did not assume that mask of frozen arrogance behind which she usually took refuge when she had been led into making confidences. In a dreamy sort of voice, she said:

"Do you remember, Edward, that's what we used to say to mamma when we were children – that she could never commit a sin? Claude. . . ." (he started at the sound of his name upon her lips) ". . . in spite of all the knowledge you have acquired, I rather think that at heart you are just a simple-minded little boy!"

Then, fearing that he might be hurt, she added:

"I mean that as a compliment."

Edward warned his sister that though Claude might think that she was sinless, he did not for a moment doubt that she would be damned along with all other heretics. The country lad protested. He could not bear people to joke on that subject. He explained, with great precision, that it was quite possible for those who were not declared members of the corporate body of the Church, to belong to it in spirit. He hated Edward's smile, hated the cruelty in his eyes, and the lassitude which showed in the drooping corners of his wide mouth. Nevertheless, he continued to talk, flattered and thrilled by the attention which May was paying to his words, and thinking that with just such an expression must Jacqueline Pascal have sat among the Jansenist doctors. When he declared that only those seek God who have already found Him, Edward broke in:

"My dear fellow, do please spare us that quotation from the Mystery of Jesus! At the point you have reached in your dissertation it never fails to produce the required effect!"

Claude averted his eyes from the mocker, and relapsed into silence.

"You mustn't be shocked," said May who, having risen to her feet, was now standing with both arms round her brother's neck: "it's a kind of shyness he suffers from whenever conversation soars. He feels that he's got to prick the bubble."

"Yes," said Edward (touching her hair with his lips) "we always make rather a point of not flogging a subject. . . ."

They both laughed. The phrase formed part of their own private language. Claude did his best to understand. It astonished him to find that he was suffering without having the slightest idea what it was that had caused his suffering, nor why he suddenly felt a longing to be alone. Edward picked up from the grass a copy of *Fleurs du Mal* which May had been reading while the two young men were bathing.

"Here," he said, "is the proper finale for an afternoon like this."

Claude knew nothing of the author's writings, except *l'Invitation au Voyage* which he had heard Mademoiselle sing. Edward proposed reading aloud, but the girl thought differently:

"Here, give it me" she said: "you're such a bad reader!"

She tried to snatch the book from him, but he ran off shaking with laughter, with her hard at his heels. They were just like two children on an afternoon of the summer holidays. Claude hoped fervently that the great revelation would be made to him through the medium of May's voice. Edward finally admitted defeat, but they must wait, he said, until his sister had recovered her breath. She read again *l'Invitation au Voyage*, and then *La Vie antérieure*, *Le Balcon*, and other poems, all in the same monotonous voice. The long grasses cast a shadow on the page. They returned home in silence. Claude watched the moon following the car from tree to tree. Madame Gonzales was waiting for them. She announced ceremoniously that Edith, her darling daughter, had unexpectedly arrived by the four o'clock train. Edward and May, who had long been prepared for this surprise, did not even go through the form of asking whether the girl was tired after her journey, or of finding out which room she had been given. Madame Gonzales, whom Edith had told not to come bothering her while she was washing, relieved her feelings by writing a long letter to Monsieur Dupont-Gunther.

"Your children," she told him, "have been bathing and romping with the Favereau boy. I am very glad of it, for he has been dogging my footsteps, though why I don't know. I'll try and worm something out of him. Finally, dear friend,

Edith has come. She's given up her job as Manageress of the
Splendid Hotel at Biarritz, where some of the guests were
beginning to show her rather too much attention. Rather than
risk being compromised she has decided to leave. You've only
got to see her to realize that nobody could help adoring her.
See you Saturday, Bertie dear."

Claude was leaning from his window in the moonlight. He
repeated to himself a line which May had taught him on the
river bank:

"*Je sais l'art d'évoquer les minutes heureuses.*"

How those simple words echoed in his mind! The sky was
so light that the cocks were waking. Happy minutes . . .
Claude longed to evoke them, to treasure them against the
long, joyless months that lay ahead. A falling star glowed and
went out. Perhaps in some other place other dreaming children
had seen it, and whispered a wish. Did it dare, poor heart,
admit the vague desire that haunted it?

VI

THE presence of Edith Gonzales diverted Edward's
attention from Claude. He was beginning to grow tired
of his uneventful existence at Lur, and her bleached hair
and painted face reminded him of Paris. He had come away in
an access of enthusiasm. After long months of emotional
excitement nothing holds so much promise of happiness as a
house in the country, solitude and silence. His meeting with
Claude had, for a few weeks, kept boredom at bay. But the
possibilities of a young country boy are soon exhausted, even

if he *is* a baby priest. Edward, therefore, had got out his paint-box and cleaned his brushes. It was only when he was left with nothing to do, and no one to amuse him, that his mind turned to thoughts of work. Art, for him, was always a last resort. None of his pictures could give him the slightest feeling of surprise. No matter whether he tried his hand at distortion, or painted what he saw before him with painstaking exactness, everything he produced was a mere exercise in technique. His painting was completely lacking in sincerity. His apples were bad Cézanne. He recognized the *provenance* of every single one of his touches on the canvas. He had no illusions about himself. Such praise as had come his way in Paris had a false ring. He was admired either for what was most mediocre in him, or for qualities which were not, strictly, his own. On the other hand, he fully subscribed to every piece of adverse criticism, and even recognized the justice of the silence and oblivion with which he was already surrounded in matters of art, which, he felt, would be his eternal lot.

Then this good-looking girl had suddenly turned up just when he had been beginning to feel that he had nothing in the world to do. The torrid heats make the emotionally undisciplined only too susceptible to the urgencies of the flesh. He hung about the newcomer whose studied attitude of indifference acted on him like a stimulant. The uneasy cluck-ings of the Gonzales hen made it perfectly clear to him that he was putting a spoke in a very secret wheel. The way in which Edith, from Saturday night to Tuesday morning was careful to have nothing to do with him, and lavished her attentions entirely on Bertie Dupont-Gunther, filled Edward with the certainty that he would be performing a pious action by troubling the still waters of this conceited young creature, this "nice handful of woman's flesh" as old Favereau described her.

And so it was that, absorbed in his adventure, he left Claude

and May to their theological discussions. May never grew
tired of questioning the former seminarist, who would very
much rather have talked with her about less abstract matters.
Nevertheless, the Christian youth had retained too many
scruples not to do his best to enlighten the worried Calvinist
maiden whose ideas on the subject of the Church were so
strange that Claude could not help growing indignant, and
put all his passion into the task of refuting them. He explained
to her the limits of Papal Infallibility, and pointed out that it
did not imply Impeccability. May was very glad to learn that
Catholics do not worship the Virgin, and that Indulgencies, the
traffic in which had precipitated the Reformation, derive from
the admirable dogma of the Communion of Saints.

Their conversations took place, as a rule, at the hour of the
day when siesta empties the fields, and the sun forces men and
beasts to seek the darkness of their lairs, there to sleep, while
it is left sole master of the vines and dusty roads. But the two
had no fear of him: maybe, they even blessed the collusive
blaze and fierceness which enveloped them in an enchanted
solitude holding them isolated at the heart of a universal
furnace. Even the Gonzales woman, who was forever on the
watch, never stirred out of her room before five, fearing that
she might get sunstroke. Claude wished, yet did not wish, to
escape from the theological disputations which were the
pretext for these meetings. Each day he decided to diverge
from such high matters, but could never bring himself to do
so. On the contrary, he confined himself within them, as
though, outside the limits of religious debate, he would find
nothing but traps and ambushes. Besides, no sooner did May
so much as get a whiff of less austere subjects of conversation,
than, with a direct question, she brought Claude back into the
straight and narrow path. At first she had done this instinctively, but later with intention, as soon as she had guessed the

nature of his longings and had felt in her own heart a threat of complicity. She sometimes wondered why she was behaving in this way, without altogether realizing that the important thing, so far as she was concerned, was to give herself an excuse, to legitimize these meetings at the bar of her own conscience, so to arrange matters that no imprudent word should make them for ever impossible. It was not that for a single moment she had ceased to be passionately interested in these pious discussions. Claude had, at first, allowed himself to be drawn into them, but, for all that, he had become absorbed. In vain did youth on either side exercise its attractions and thrill their emotions. They had got to talk of these things. To the obscure drama of the flesh, someone had succeeded, someone who overtopped it.

Claude appeared in the doorway of the hall, clutching to his breast a bundle of reeds cut from the frog-pond, the noise of which each evening made Madame Gonzales regret the days when serfs had swept the castle moats free of all animal life.
"Ah! that's what we need!" exclaimed the lady, who was crouching on the billiard-table from which she could reach the porcelain ceiling-lamp. She was stretching her plump little arms above her crooked "transformation", but they were too short. Edward and May raised their eyes from the album at which they were looking, sketched the semblance of a smile, and exchanged a look which Edith Gonzales, seated on the sofa opposite, just caught out of the corner of her eye. Finally, she abandoned her odalisque pose, climbed in her turn on to the billiard-table, and took over the task from her mother who, with a loud sigh, announced that she gave it up, and, collapsing on to the sofa, proceeded to fan herself with a large handkerchief which she always said was the one she kept for when she had a cold in the head.

"Will you be needing me any longer, ma'am?" asked Claude, who knew full well that he would be called back as soon as he had reached the terrace steps.

"Need you any longer? . . ." (she fixed him with a vacant stare, her thoughts being elsewhere) ". . . do we want any more flowers, May?"

She pointed her lorgnette at the girl who was with her brother on the sofa where the two of them gave the appearance of being on the "other side" as in a game of prisoners'-base. May replied that she really didn't care what flowers they had, and continued to work through the album with the carefully assumed air of one who was completely dissociated from all the feverish arrangements now going forward.

Edward and May knew perfectly well why the Castagnède family had been invited. Ever since her sixteenth year the girl had been besieged by the tenacious but timid desires of Marcel Castagnède, whom no rebuff, no evidences of disdain, could long discourage. It had been only necessary for Madame Gonzales to be made privy to some project entertained by Monsieur Gunther, for the secret to leak out, even though she never breathed a word. It seemed to ooze from her imposing presence. At meal-times she had a way, apropos of nothing, of turning the conversation to the subject of the Castagnède family, of saying suddenly, that Marcel Castagnède's eyes were quite the most beautiful she had ever seen. . . .

"Would you like to come down and have a look at the dahlias?" ventured Edith Gonzales with an affable smile.

May said she felt tired, and, two minutes later, made her rudeness worse by asking Edward whether he would like to take a turn with her in the garden.

Claude, forgetful of good manners, was standing in the middle of the room, his arms dangling, deeply interested by a drama with the undercurrents of which he was familiar from having heard the matter discussed among the servants. Madame Gonzales was on familiar terms with her maid, and the members of the staff were well posted in their employers' concerns. He would have stayed there still longer had not Madame Gonzales dismissed him with a – "You can go now, young man" – words in which there was an ominous threat of thunder.

The sultry afternoon was strangely still and silent. There was a slate-grey colour about the horizon which, framed in the dark green foliage of the hornbeam alley, appeared to be rising higher and higher, and to be progressively encroaching on, and staining, the blue of the sky.

Edward and May, too, got to their feet and walked away side by side, without saying a word. Seeing Claude at some distance from them, employed in weeding the path which bordered the "view", they did their best to avoid him, and, in spite of the oppressive heat, made off in the direction of the vines.

"What a life!" murmured May. "We've had just about as much as we can stand, don't you think, Edward? . . . and now, to crown all, I'm faced by this renewed Marcel Castagnède persecution."

She almost hissed the last few words. Edward said nothing. The evil grin which she knew so well was stretching the corners of her brother's mouth, making his whole face ugly. Into his eyes, too, had come the wicked, equivocal glitter which, when she was a little girl had always made her say – "stop looking like a crazy cat!" – for his expression at such moments had rather too much of their father in it.

"My dear girl, let's not dramatize everything, please. You do enjoy a bit of drama in your life, don't you?"

"How hard you are to-day, Edward." Her eyes filled with tears, for pride was of no avail when she was at odds with her brother. Edward showed no sign of softening, but, in the same cutting tones, remarked that it was only too clear that he was in for a rhodomontade in the grand manner.

May came to a halt. A huge storm cloud had by this time covered all the sky. There was a sudden puff of hot wind. The swallows were skimming almost at grass level. The screech and scrape of insects had grown shriller.

"I think we'd better be getting back," she said. "After all, it was for my sake – or so I thought – that you came to Lur, to help me because I should be all alone here. . . ."

She was crying. Gone now was every trace of the impassive countenance with which she faced her father's fury and Madame Gonzales' heavy-handed treacheries. The wind had slightly disarranged her hair. With her swollen eyes, and her face all puckered like a little girl's, she looked so pitiful, so plain, that Edward felt amazed at his inability to feel sorry for her, to feel, indeed, anything that might have shattered the solid block within him of cold unconcern, disgust and boredom. This was one of his bad days.

Without making a movement, without uttering a word, he watched her walk away towards the alley. She crossed the terrace, almost at a run, her head down, in the teeth of the south wind which dried her tears and pricked her eyelids. At a turn in the path she ran into Claude. Overcome by embarrassment, she could only stammer a few words:

"I think there's a storm coming up. It won't belong before it breaks."

Claude made no attempt to answer. With his mouth half open, and his great hands hanging at his sides, he stared at her. He wiped away the moisture from his streaming forehead with his sleeve, then looked again at the miserable face before him. May hurried on, appalled by what she had seen in his eyes – a fierce ardour of compassion, and (she could dare now to admit it to herself) – of love. She fled to her room, where the Venetian blinds were still down, and stretched herself at length on the *chaise-longue* with its delicious chitzy smell. She told herself that she had come here to suffer in silence. For some odd reason, however, she was not suffering at all. On the contrary, in spite of misgivings, melancholy, and hatred, she was filled with a shameful emotion of joy because she knew that he loved her, joy in which anguish played a part, and, more especially, humiliation. For all that, joy predominated.

When his sister had disappeared, Edward sat down between two rows of vines, facing the plain. With his face between his hands, he tried to look into his heart. 'It is true,' he said to himself, 'that I did come here to give her my support, but also true that at this precise moment nothing to do with her is of the slightest interest to me.' He had long been aware of the hateful quirk in his character which could suddenly make him lose all concern for things and people who had a short while before deeply occupied his mind and engaged his feelings, so that where there had been what had appeared to be a deeply rooted emotion, there was nothing now but a hole, an utter emptiness. 'What a complete rotter I am,' he reflected. 'I know perfectly well that if I suddenly felt an itch to go – oh, anywhere, to a music-hall with its complement of tarts – anywhere at all, on the hunt for adventure, I am perfectly capable of abandoning her, even though I am quite certain she is miserable, without the slightest compunction. But I'm *not* going away: I'm staying on here. I don't feel any desire to go, though what on earth's keeping me I haven't the slightest idea. Lur's got dam' little to offer.'

He was not left wondering for long. At first he thought that Claude might be the attraction. The casual encounter that he represented was the kind of thing he most thoroughly enjoyed. He let his mind brood for a moment or two on the fact that

Claude was in love with May, and also on the feeling of friendship which he knew that he had aroused in that young and guileless heart. Yes, that was all very charming, but there was something even more so. Edith Gonzales had been in the house for only a week. She had been brought there for a definite purpose, the nature of which her mother believed that nobody knew. But, from the very first minute, he had guessed it. The girl intrigued him mightily, as did the manoeuvres in which she was engaged. As he had watched her hanging round Bertie in obedience to the demands of her mother's crude diplomacy, his feeling at first had been one of surprise at the skill with which Edith was exploiting the situation, and at the rapidity with which Bertie had snapped at the proffered bait. But a little later he had been astonished to see that Edith was beginning to neglect her duty, was showing signs that her mind was not on her work. She had snubbed the old gentleman once or twice rather more obviously than was altogether wise – and all because she had let her eyes light upon him, Edward.

'This struggle *à la Corneille* between love and duty,' he said to himself '(granted that her duty in this cases consists in seducing the master of the house, and her love in being seduced by me) has the makings of a most amusing situation.'

He was not sufficiently sincere to take the further step, and say 'I find it, I don't mind admitting, extremely flattering.' All the same, it was! Edward had that combined look of physical fitness and temperamental sensitiveness which is, as it were, the hall-mark of the undergraduate of Magdalen College. Nevertheless, he had never had much "luck" with women. Perhaps he lacked simplicity, the gift of unconditional surrender. No woman had ever yet been able to delude herself into thinking that she could dominate him, could make herself necessary to his happiness. He was always a thousand miles removed from female preoccupations. What it all amounted to was that he could neither give pleasure nor be content to accept it. He was a moody creature if ever there was one. No sooner had he involved himself in a escapade than he was all eagerness to find a way out. Women, in his view, were good for one thing only: 'apart from that' he told himself, 'they bore me.' He dreaded their laughter, their chatter, the aimless agitations with which they filled their lives. He took not the slightest interest in either their servants or their dressmakers. As to the serious-minded, the blue-stockings, they got on his nerves to an even greater extent. What he really enjoyed was a life of endless talk and discussion with young men of his own age.

"If ever I kill myself," he had once said: "it certainly won't be for a woman. Fancy wanting to die because one happens to be in love! that ought to be an additional reason for wanting to stay alive! One commits suicide because one's got nothing left – not even that!" It was along these lines that his thoughts were running now, as he stared at the dark horizon. To be sure, no woman's manoeuvres had ever amused him more than did Edith's: but even they did not count for much in his life. The pleasure he got from watching them were no greater than he might find in a well-made play.

'Not that I'm not interested in them – or in Claude, too, for that matter – but that's only because for the moment there's nothing else for me to hold on to.'

This was a favourite expression of his. He liked to compare himself to a man suspended over an abyss, and clinging for safety to a branch or a plank. Each time he felt the slightest stirring of love or friendship, he convinced himself that the new emotion was all that stood between him and death.

'If the time should ever come when I had left Edith and Claude alone together in a room at Aix or Biarritz, and an open window happened to be handy, it's then that I. . . .'

Over and over again he had rehearsed the details of a possible suicide, going so far as to imagine the paragraphs in the papers, the look on his father's face, to hear May's cry, to compute the degrees of indifference in the way in which his friends would react to the news.

He rose to his feet, and moved away down the path along which his sister had fled. How surprisingly silent the birds were! Except for the immense vibration of a myriad hidden insects, the only sound that reached him was the tap of steel on stone which came from the spot where Claude was busy weeding. Dragging his sandalled feet, Edward continued on his way, his head slightly raised because the wind was blowing the smoke of his cigarette into his eyes. The smile which May so much disliked gave an ugly look to a face which had suddenly become old and vicious. On reaching the pleached alley he could have diverged towards the house. That, he knew, would have been the wisest course, for he had nothing to say to Claude that would not hurt his feelings. But an irresistible attraction led him in the young man's direction. Claude had already straightened up and was smiling at him from a distance. They began by exchanging a few common-places about the failure of the storm to break. Then, without a word of warning, Claude said:

"You must forgive me, Mr. Edward, for talking about matters that don't concern me, but I couldn't help noticing, when your sister passed me a while back, how terribly sad she looked. . . ."

There was in the look he turned on Edward a wordless appeal for aid, but that maliciously inclined young gentleman was getting far too much amusement from the situation to take any active steps. He merely thanked the other for taking so much interest in his sister. Perhaps she had something on her mind, something quite trivial, no doubt.

But Claude would not let the subject alone:

"Then may I take it that you're not worried?"

"My dear Claude, I don't feel like being worried about anything or anybody."

Claude frowned, as he always did when he was brought up short by one of Edward's strange moods: the very sound of his voice, at such times, seemed to baffle him. He scarcely recognized the face he thought he knew.

"Oh! Mister Edward, I can't help feeling you wouldn't talk like that if you didn't feel easy in your mind."

"Claude, Claude," said Edward, "you are guilty of an error which may bring you much unhappiness. You believe that some things in life are really important!"

Claude replied that he regarded everything in life as important, because each one of our most trivial gestures, each one of our most secret thoughts, is revealed to the eyes of God.

He had an uncomfortable feeling that Edward could read him better than he could read himself, and that what he had never dared to admit in his most secret broodings had for some time been a source of amusement to his young masters. He said nothing, therefore. Edward embarked, almost immediately, on a stream of nonsensical chatter. It must be vastly entertaining, he said, to be able to watch all the twists and turns of a family drama from the viewpoint of the servants' hall. Had he, himself, been born in humbler circumstances, he could have found no pleasanter way of passing the time than in being one of those over-fed footmen who hang about the halls and stairs of great houses on the occasion of big dinner parties, for they have more opportunity than ever Balzac had, of knowing all about the guests. But if one was to get the best out of the situation it was essential to remain, so to speak, in the wings, and not to mingle with the actors on the stage, or attempt to play a part oneself. Claude, he said, was not making full use of his good fortune, which could enable him to indulge in a good laugh at the expense of the grotesque characters who haunted this tumble-down mansion.

The sound of the rake falling from the poor lad's hands, made him stop, Claude had gone so pale that, for the first time, Edward noticed a few patches of freckles on his nose and cheeks. Drops of rain were spattering the leaves, and the smell of the earth rose in the damp air.

Edward made off at a run. From the hall, Edith Gonzales, her forehead pressed to the window, watched him coming. Had he caught cold? she asked. He told her to keep away from him, because the smell of wet cloth sometimes made people feel faint. He enquired whether the Castagnède family had turned up yet.

"No: but it's time we started to get ready. I'll go upstairs with you."

They reached the staircase, which was dark because of the storm, and started up, Edith leading. He noticed that the hair grew in an ugly way at the nape of her neck. 'It's a common neck' – he told himself. He noticed, too, on the white skin a circlet of puckers. In less than five years, he reflected, her cheeks would begin to sag, and there would be indications of a double chin. She would look almost an old woman. Her wrists had lost the freshness of youth already, and very soon the veins upon her hands would be prominent. She had good reason to conceal her temples. . . . Edith climbed very slowly, convinced that what she felt upon her neck was the hot breath of desire. As she got near the first landing, she slowed her pace even more, waiting until the breath should reach her hair, and be transformed into a kiss. Edward guessed what she was thinking, and, not to disappoint her, took her forearms in his two hands. She seemed flustered, and her neck swelled like a turtle-dove's. But in the dim light she could see Edward's sharp eyes and cruel face. Instinctively, she turned away her own. The young man did not insist, but whispered in her ear that he admired her presence of mind.

"You've remembered, just in time, that you didn't come here to amuse yourself."

She leaned on the banister rail. Her face was hidden from him, but he could imagine its expression of shame and anger.

"I don't know what you mean! You're hateful! let me alone!"

A door on the landing opened, and Madame Gonzales appeared, tightly swathed in a glittering dress of steel spangles which revealed all that, in the daytime, could be seen only piecemeal through the soft fabric of her blouse. One fat, short arm, adorned with a dog-collar bracelet with one or two of the pearls missing, was holding aloft a candlestick which threw its light down on Edith and Edward.

"Not dressed yet?" she said tartly. Her great bilious face remined Edward of Napoleon as he might have looked, on the eve of battle, having discovered that an order had not been carried out correctly.

"Hurry! hurry! you stupid girl!" Then, without addressing a word to Edward, and with much clicking of steel and jet, she went downstairs, pulling a pair of too narrow gloves over her powdered arms.

"Your lady mother," said Edward, "reminds me of the end of one of Baudelaire's sonnets."

Edith shrugged, and went into her room. Edward, too, went to his, repeating to himself with relish, the three lines which, for him, represented the *leit-motif* of the Gonzales family:

> Je vois ta mère, enfant de ce siècle appauvri,
> Qui vers son miroir penche un lourd amas d'années
> Et plâtre artistement le sein qui t'a nourri

He lit his brass lamp, passed his hand lovingly over the cool earthenware vase which was like a pebble smoothed by running water. The gold in the Persian shawl glittered. Like some prince who, visiting a foreign city, recovers his sense of sovereignty within the embassy walls, he breathed in here the atmosphere of the Paris he knew. He filled his bath with a feverish pleasure which reminded him of one of those evenings when, before going out, he had made a careful toilet so as to be ready for any eventuality, any adventure.

Seated in the hot water with his arms clasped about his knees, he thought: 'What can I dare hope for in this desert?' Was it not this attitude of expectancy which gave him the strength never to sink forever, this need he felt not to fall short of the smallest chance of casual pleasure?

He heard the purring of a car, the louder volume of sound as it changed gear, a burst of laughter, the prattle of voices. In front of the three-sided glass, as in the days of his youth when he had wanted to give the impression that he was extraordinarily young, he shaved himself so closely that he almost drew blood, and, because he was so very fair, looked suddenly no more than eighteen. He filled a silver case with cigarettes, and slipped a platinum wrist-watch on to his arm. He forgot the financial, and other, more obscure, reasons which made his father want to see May satisfactorily married. He refused to let himself think about his sister's misery, or about the struggle in which she must be involved. All that mattered to him was to please, to unsettle, Edith, and to bring into her eyes the glint he knew so well. Even the presence of the Castagnède family did not displease him. He was expecting to get a deal of quiet amusement from the spectacle of fat Marcel in love. The meeting, too, of old mother Castagnède and the Gonzales woman, promised a certain amount of rather grotesque entertainment.

There was still an hour before dinner, and, since he had no intention of enduring a long tête-a-tête with the Castagnèdes, Edward gave a wide berth to the chatter in the drawing-room, threw a light coat over his shoulders, and went back to the terrace where he came unexpectedly on Claude who, at sight of him, tried to slip away.

"Did I startle you?" asked Edward.

"You are too complicated. . . . Oh, I realize that one shouldn't take your mockeries all that seriously, but what you said just now hurt me."

He was afraid that Edward might burst out laughing. On the contrary, the young man assumed a serious expression.

"It is true, Claude, that between us two there is a great gulf fixed. I am not talking of social differences, but of a spiritual distance. I can have only a bad influence on you, and you can do nothing for me."

"That is not true, Mr. Edward: I can suffer for you."

It was the old seminarist in him that prompted this instinctive answer. Edward knew all about the mystical doctrine of substitution. He said:

"I have no wish, dear boy, that you should be my scapegoat, nor that you should assume the burden of my crimes."

Claude was amazed by the words that came to his lips:

"I will take them upon myself, should that really be your wish."

It was as though somebody else were speaking in his place. Edward was enchanted by the prospect of so strange a pact. Though he had no belief in its effectiveness, like all superstitious persons, he could not help being impressed. He grasped Claude's hand:

"I accept your offer. From now on I can enjoy myself to my heart's content, can't I? You're the one who will pay the price of my spiritual – and other – orgies of self-indulgence. . . ."

His big mouth, distended by laughter, revealed two canine teeth. Claude was suddenly conscious of a secret feeling of repulsion for the man. He felt released from his attraction . . . what matter if he had to suffer later?

"I will take this opportunity, Claude, of saying good-bye. Nobody knows as yet that I shall soon be leaving Lur. I very much wonder whether I shall ever come back. . . ."

With a sneering laugh, which might have meant anything, he added:

"Don't worry . . . May's staying. . . ."

With a careless air he made off towards the lighted drawing-room. Claude hoped that he would never see him again, nor hear the sound of his voice. He drove from his mind the memory of the pact which he had just made. Nevertheless, he was conscious of a weight of uneasiness. He felt that some unsatisfied, some unappeasable, spirit of malice was prowling round his destined future.

VII

EDWARD'S entry into the drawing-room broke the agonising constriction of a general silence. He saw the faces of all those present turn, at the same moment, towards him under the wonderfully soft irradiation of oil lamps and candles in their crystal lustres. But the look of disappointment with which his arrival was greeted, made it clear that somebody was still missing. His sister was in no haste to come down. The sound of her dawdling footsteps on the floor above was distinctly audible. The last of the daylight was still filtering into the room through the open windows, and mingled with the lamps to produce a sort of mortuary glow. Madame Castagnède occupied the whole of one of the "poufs". Her head and face, with its grey hair and sagging cheeks, rose straight out of her shoulders. Her neck was so almost non-existent that the collar of diamonds she was wearing seemed as though it had been but there to conceal the stitches of a join. Two enormous "drops" weighed down her old ears. Her very obvious wig showed a line of tight curls above her eyebrows, and mingled, half way down the back of her neck, with a few natural grey hairs. She offered her hand to Edward in a manly handshake, but he touched it lightly with respectful and ironic lips. He turned to Marcel Castagnède, and put into his "How are you, old man?" all the disdain to which the other had been accustomed since their schooldays. Marcel had inherited from his mother a thickening waistline, but his doglike eyes of a deep brown were frank and honest. His half-open mouth showed strong, but irregular teeth. He had a sloping forehead and next to no chin. His wide shoulders gave him an air of poise. He looked clean and fresh, and had that pleasantly healthy appearance which comes of open-air sports and frequent baths. It took very little to make him blush.

The gravel of the drive grated under the wheels of a victoria, the lamps of which showed briefly in the darkness, gleaming on the leaves of a laurel bush which stood close beside the open window. Monsieur Dupont-Gunther took obvious pleasure in announcing the arrival of his excellent friend and neighbour, Firmin Pacaud. His purple chops rested on an excessively starched collar. Turning towards Madame Castagnède, he said: "Old Pacaud's presence will, I feel sure, not mar the intimacy of this family party."

He pointed these last words with a significant smile. Madame Castagnède did not turn a hair, but merely remarked that the family party still lacked one of its most charming components. This reference to May's inexplicable failure to appear increased the general embarrassment. Fortunately, at this moment, Firmin Pacaud came into the room. He was a man of forty-five with a beard, a paunch, and brushed-back hair. Though the sunburn on his hands and on a bald patch on his head, denoted the countryman, his much-worn smoking jacket and cracked pumps were those of a man of the world. Edward went swiftly across to Monsieur Pacaud who smiled blissfully as soon as, the formal politenesses ended, he could devote his whole attention to the young man, to whose charm he was extremely susceptible. Edward like him because he had remained young in heart and mind, and was quite free of all professional idiosyncrasies. He greeted him as usual:

"How goes it, Dominique?"

"Why always 'Dominique,' you young rascal?"

"Because, my dear fellow, Firmin is an impossible name."

"I don't think so" said Madame Gonzales, with an appallingly genteel smile which revealed a flash of golden fillings.

"Firmin is an impossible name" reiterated Edward, in a tone which expelled this female intrusion from their talk. "Another reason why I call you Dominique is that I always think Fromentin's hero must have looked like you."

Pacaud pretended to be offended. "You mean I suppose, that you regard me as an intelligent and sympathetic failure, eh?"

"Far from it: I regard you as a mature man who can still indulge in dreams. You have managed, dear old friend, to steer clear of experience and of the crippling effects of your job, of everything, in short, that makes men of your age as a rule so terribly boring."

"And yet, we're utterly different, you and I. For all our mutual affection, we don't share a single taste in poetry or music."

"Of course! I may call you Dominique, but really, don't you think you're much more like one of Bourget's early heroes – Armand de Querne, for instance, in *Crime d'Amour*?"

"Alexandre Dumas' *Ami des Femmes* would be nearer the mark! I've always been very partial to the fair sex!"

"So have I"

"Damme, yes – you can take your pleasure with them (though you have others, too) but you don't live for women, as I did . . . I suppose that, in all, they must have run me into something like four hundred thousand francs, one way and another, but I don't regret it. The famous Burdeau was in philosophy class with me at Louis-le-Grand, and almost all my schoolfellows have made names for themselves. Like them, I could have done something in journalism or politics, might have counted for quite a lot among those who make a large splash in a little puddle – but I preferred love, and I don't care if you *do* laugh!"

"Why should I laugh? I'm someone who's never made a sacrifice for anything."

Edward's face had clouded over. He raised his shoulders in a shrug, and looked so depressed and miserable that Monsieur Pacaud felt like grasping his hand.

Madame Gonzales' fan was making a continuous clicking sound against the steel and jet ornaments of her corsage. Madame Castagnède was studying one of her gloves which had split between the fingers. Monsieur Gunther said something that sounded more like a bark than anything else, and, while it echoed round the room, frowned as he tried to think of some other remark to make. Marcel Castagnède addressed to Edith the same series of questions he had trotted out ever since he had begun going to parties, and in precisely the same order: "Are you fond of reading, Mademoiselle? Personally, I adore being by myself . . . and of music? Personally, I don't pretend to understand Wagner. . . . Have you done much travelling. . . . hotels are awfully comfortable nowadays. . . . Which do you like best, the sea or the mountains? The sea is always the same, and yet it isn't, if you understand what I mean. I've seen lots of sunsets at Royan. If a painter produced all those different colours one would say he was an Impressionist." Marcel made all these remarks, one after the other, in a never changing order, as a penitent catalogues his sins in the confessional. All the same, he was keeping his eyes fixed on the door through which May must come, unless, of course, she sent down some excuse, and didn't appear at all.

Firmin Pacaud thoughtlessly put into words what everyone was thinking:

"Our little May's keeping us waiting rather a long time this evening."

Monsieur Gunther's hands were trembling, and, as usual, he kept them behind his back.

"This really is too much," he growled: "go up and see what she's doing, Edward."

But, in the silence following this outburst, a rustle became audible behind the door, and, next moment, the girl appeared upon the threshold. She stood there for a few seconds stock still. Her dress was of the sulphur yellow to be seen in certain types of rose. She was wearing an Indian bracelet, and a tiny edging of under-bodice was showing at her breast, as happens with young girls when they have no mother to give them a final look-over.

Edward saw that her hands were clenched, and that she was smiling. He was surprised that her face was not a mask of tragedy. 'She looks only half here,' he said to himself: 'like a sleep-walker in a happy dream. . . .' He was still more surprised when he saw her, with the same vague and tender smile upon her lips, take Marcel Castagnède's arm. 'Wonder whether she's given herself a shot of morphine? Could she have got hold of some coke without my knowing?' He was perfectly well aware that in one of her recurring moods of desperation, May was capable of the most lunatic excesses.

Marcel was seated next to her at dinner. He was profoundly happy because the loved-one listened to him in so docile a fashion, even though she *did* seem a little bit remote, and answered him without, apparently, thinking what she was saying. But it was enough for him that she was not disdainful.

But May, in fact, was hearing nothing, seeing nothing. The proud young creature had confessed to herself, had dared to confess, that she was happy, happy because a young man loved her. Nothing could take her mind from that delight, nor from the pleasure she felt in conjuring up endlessly within her mind the picture of Claude's worn and wasted face. Edward himself had said that there was one thing only in the world that could make life worth living – to give a boundless love to one who loves boundlessly in return. That one thing would be hers!

Contrary to her usual habit, she drained her glass of Johannisberger, and another of Laffitte, just so that they might be refilled. She felt within herself an uprush of life. She could pursue a conversation with Marcel, and yet, all the time, be giving herself to a burning dialogue in which question and answer followed one another in her mind which now she felt was utterly freed from bondage. . . . 'I was,' she thought, 'like a little girl who thinks that she is imprisoned within a circle drawn upon the sand.' She concentrated her every effort on conjuring up Claude as she had seen him last, comparing his glowing, healthy body with Marcel's load of fat, with Edward's moroseness. She even found a pleasure, proud little Huguenot that she was, in the humiliation of loving a social inferior whose secret kingliness she alone could see. 'So much purity, so much knowledge, so much physical passion in one and the same person!' she thought. What, by comparison, did Edward's inability to feel anything matter, that taste of his for nothingness, which, sooner or later, would lead him to suicide, "for" she said out loud, "he will most certainly kill himself."

"There you are wrong, Mademoiselle: Bombita will never kill himself: he knows his job too well."

Marcel was describing a bull-fight he had seen at Saint-Sebastian. May felt as though she had woken up with a start. She looked at her neighbour. They were sitting so close together that she could have counted the drops of sweat on the receding forehead. The ugliness of all the faces round the table frightened her. Gladly and unnoticed she withdrew within her dream, soundlessly playing over the *Death of Isolde*, hearing the harps, drawing to herself the mounting tide of mortal anguish told in song. Once again the secret tempest rose and swelled, like a tide of death, until it reached its climax in one final, breathless cry: and so vivid was all this that, when they went back to the drawing-room she, who, as a rule was so fierce in her refusal to play for anybody, broke of her own accord into the flow of conversation:

"Would you like some music?"

There was a general murmur of eagerness, Marcel opened the piano: Firmin Pacaud looked out a piece, and Bertie leaned towards Madame Gonzales, whispering:

"This is better than I could have hoped!"

"Indeed it is," murmured that enigmatic female.

Madame Castagnède took her seat, assumed the completely expressionless look which she wore at concerts, prepared to nod her head in time with the music, and to ask, at each pause, whether that was the end.

Edward, filled with curiosity, watched his sister go to the window. She whispered into the darkness – "will he know that I am singing for him?" then, went to the piano, took from the stand the Preludes which Firmin Pacaud had spread out, and chose from the rack the *Death of Isolde*. Firmin protested. Wagner was tolerable only when played by a full orchestra. What she had chosen ill suited a Louis-Philippe drawing-room and an old French garden. May smiled. His words had not penetrated her mind. A chord spread, and those present had the feeling that it filled the night, the vast spaces, and that these waves of agonising passion, each destroying each, were mounting to the indifferent stars. When the tempest of sound had died away, May still sat at the keyboard. A palpable sense of uneasiness was in the room. Marcel ventured a compliment:

"What mastery! One could swear she was a professional!"

In a flat voice, and as though she were speaking in her sleep, May announced:

"And now I am going to sing."

At the first words of *l'Invitation au Voyage*, Edward alone felt no surprise. He smiled: he had understood.

She shut the piano, and, once more indifferent to any effect her behaviour might produce, went and leaned against the window. A cloud of tobacco smoke hung about the blue curtains. The processes of digestion made all the old faces in the room hideous. It was not hard to imagine that Monsieur Dupont-Gunther's inevitable stroke might take place here and now. Madame Gonzales was dabbing her face with powder in a corner, but her cheeks were so red that anyone might have been justified in thinking that the plaster surface concealed a running sore. Madame Castagnède made an imperative sign to Marcel. He went across to May, who was still standing motionless, looking out into the shadowed garden. He leaned against the wall close to her, but she did not even notice his proximity. Monsieur Gunther directed at Madame Castagnède what he meant to be a sentimental smile. . . . The young

man, after long pondering how he should break the ice, at last
brought out:

"Isn't it a lovely night?"

May gave a start, looked for a moment at the great crimson
face beside her, and then shook her head as though chasing
away a fly.

The young man thanked her for having been so kind to him.

"Was I kind?" she asked: "it really wasn't intentional, you
know."

Fearing some blunder on his part, Madame Castagnède told
her son to fetch the car. Edith and Edward had gone with
Firmin Pacaud to his carriage, and had not come back. Madame
Gonzales, standing at the top of the steps, called to her daughter
in Spanish. What she said might well have been something
coarse. All the frogs stopped croaking at the same moment.
At last Edith appeared, laughing, and with her hair disordered.
Behind her, Edward's cigarette danced like a fire-fly.

That same evening, which was the 15th August, Claude, as
soon as he had finished his meal, went to the terrace. Short-
lived rockets flared and died over the distant vineyards where
whole families were celebrating name days on the Feast of
Mary. There was music in the air. He recognised it. Faithfully
it travelled towards him and found its way to the heart whither
a young girl was speeding it. The scraping of insects provided
a continuous bass. Claude gazed up at the shooting stars dying
out in the August darkness streaked by lost meteors. He
listened to the voice as though it were bringing to him some
part at least of an inaccessible body. He shed tears, thinking of
the picture he had seen in the drawing-room, showing May
and Edward with their curly heads close together. 'They will
forget me,' he thought: 'they owe me nothing. For a moment
they leaned over me, and because of them I have known something which has given an infinite value to my poor life. The

day they smiled at me, an unknown world of feelings and sweetness opened before my eyes. Whatever may happen to me, be you for ever blessed, you two young creatures, dear beings for ever beyond my reach, and may God bless you!'

He heard the sound of footsteps in the alley, saw the white glimmer of a dress, the gleam of a shirt-front, the glow of a cigarette. It was surely May he was about to see, leaning on the arm of a stranger, all sweet consent. He withdrew quickly behind some hazel bushes, not minding that his face was scratched. The wind felt colder, and his cheeks were wet. What wild relief when he recognized the voice as Edward's!

"The insolence with which you have been treating me all evening, Edith, is nothing but a wretched effort to escape. You know that I do not easily allow myself to be a prey to feeling."

Edith leaned her head on the young man's shoulder, and Claude imagined, rather than saw, her white and palpitating throat. He peered between the leaves with hungry eyes. Madame Gonzales' shrill voice sent the young people hurrying back to the house. The headlights of a car ravished the darkness, and, in the silence, Claude could hear the purring of the engine for a long while. One day the stranger would come back, and not depart again without "her" . . . Claude spoke the beloved name . . . then his thoughts turned to the seminary with its calm and uneventful days, its peace. The smell of dying roses filled the night, just as the chapel had done when, as he remembered, he used to stay on there after the others had gone. Then another thought came to him, the thought of one of his friends who had died at fifteen, one evening in June, in a quivering agony.

VIII

NOT the steaming chocolate, nor the buttered toast, nor the early sunlight shining on the tumbled bed-clothes, could keep Monsieur Gunther from reading yet again the anonymous letter in which he was informed that Mademoiselle Rosa Subra, his mistress, was having a game with him; that Juste, Monsieur Gunther's "Man", was own cousin to the lady in question; that there had been a lot of talk about them in their native village of Saint-Macaire, even when he had been a butcher's boy of fifteen, and she a servant at the Inn; that if Monsieur Gunther would not believe what was told him without first having the evidence of his own eyes, there was a friend ready to provide him, free and for nothing, with a most enjoyable spectacle.

Monsieur Gunther was choking with fury: but, suddenly, in the looking-glass opposite he caught sight of his purple cheeks and bloodshot eyes. Last night's dinner was still lying heavy on his stomach. He could feel that his blood pressure was rising. It was only terror of death that kept him from falling a victim to one of those terrible outbursts which once had filled his house with wailing and gnashing of teeth. Feeling thoroughly frightened, he unbuttoned his shirt, and plunged his hand into the great pelt which covered his chest. His heart was beating wildly. He got up, plunged his face into a basin of water, snorted loudly, then, automatically, chose a long black cigar, which he held to his ear, rolling it in his fingers to make it crackle. But just as he was about to light it he remembered his doctor's warning – no smoking on an empty stomach. How appalled he was by the thought of death! It was beyond his power to imagine that a day would come when he would no longer be able to enjoy his women, for to that pleasure he had sacrificed everything. Books and newspapers left him cold. He even regarded his business only as a means of providing him with money with which to gratify his appetites. Good food meant nothing to him except a means of stimulating for a brief while the lusts of his body. To be deprived of "that" for all eternity! He felt inclined to scream. Besides, from his Huguenot and cossetted childhood he had inherited a legacy of vague theological terrors. A long and crapulous life of self-indulgence had left him with an uneasy conscience, and he was convinced that God would be waiting for him at some turning-point of his filthy old age.

He dressed, and went down to the garden. The air was already stifling. The birds were beginning to fall silent and the insects to scrape. He heard the sound of a rake coming from the direction of the pleached alley. He saw Claude who was resting for a moment against the balustrade of the terrace. With gloomy jealousy Monsieur Gunther took in the athletic lines of the young body. Then, suddenly, his fury burst its bounds.

"What d'you think you're doing, you damned slacker! I don't pay you to day-dream! You're not in your seminary here! If you want to loaf, you'd better get back to your priests!"

Claude went a fiery red, but spoke not a word. The mere fact of his youth, he felt, was vengeance enough – better than a blow directed at this sixty-year-old. He returned to his raking. From under the turned-down brim of his sun hat he watched May, who was seated on a near-by bench reading a book the pages of which the breeze was gently fluttering. This morning he had seen her white linen frock draw near to him and then turn away. They had exchanged no more than a greeting and

a smile, but to feel in that smile of hers even the merest hint of
tenderness was bliss enough for him. She remained close by,
and he was almost sick with happiness. The reason she had not
come closer still was that Madame Gonzales was on the prowl,
armed with her lorgnette as with a double-barrelled gun. It
was ten o'clock. Heavy butterflies were coming to rest upon the
grass. The clover heads were bending under the weight of
bees. On the bark of a lime tree a cicada was climbing upwards with the sun. For May the sound of a man raking gravel
filled the great silence of the world. Furtively, she looked at
Claude's open shirt: she longed to lean her cheek against his
chest: would a young Catholic girl include such a wish in her
confession? How tired she was of being her own law-giver!
If only, from now on, her heart could just respond, like those
butterflies, to every breeze, like those drunken bees, to every
scent! Once again Madame Gonzales' orange parasol came
into view. Her stomach was constricted within a dress of
unbleached linen. For the moment she was not engaged in
spying, but was hurrying along without stretched neck like an
over-size hen which had caught sight of an insect in the distance.
She was making her way towards the vines through which
Monsieur Gunther was striding like a madman. She
approached him, and said how pleased she was that yesterday's
little occasion had gone off so very much better than might
have been expected in view of May's quite appalling character.
Monsieur Gunther uttered a coarse word which made it clear
that he did not give a damn for the little occasion. She studied
him carefully, and led the way back to the house which was
filled with the smell of stale cigar smoke.

"Something's worrying you, isn't it, my friend? tell me all
about it."

Monsieur Gunther, without uttering a word, handed her
the anonymous letter which she read, as actresses do on the

stage, with an incredible rapidity, from which it might have been inferred that she already knew what it contained. Then she folded it up and put it away in her handbag.

"My poor dear! I only wish I could tell you it was a parcel of lies!"

"But you can't, Mélanie, is that what you mean?"

"Yes, I'm afraid I can't. Oh, Bertie! you know what you once were to me, but my devotion to your interests is far greater than my pride, and if only I could believe that Rosa Subra would make you happy. . . ."

Monsieur Gunther shouted her down. It was she, he stormed, who had introduced the girl to him, and that wasn't much to be grateful for!

Madame Gonzales heaved a sigh: "I realize now that I was deceived in her. What a child you are! Why should you get into such a state? you know you don't love her."

Monsieur Gunther was in a furious temper. What did she know about it? he roared.

She remained calm and collected. "I know *you*," she replied, and then, lowering her voice, murmured:

"I know your little ways." She had, in fact, good reason for not being ignorant of them.

"Besides," she went on: "Rosa is far from young."

"She is thirty," said Monsieur Gunther, suddenly quieting down and showing an interest in the conversation.

"She's thirty-eight if she's a day, my dear. Why on earth do you want to cling to an idiotic creature who is within measurable distance of being an old woman, who is costing you the earth, who deceives you with a servant, and keeps you in a constant state of agitation which the doctor says is the worst possible thing for you?"

Quite shamelessly, Bertie demanded whether she had anything better to offer him. In her – "what do you take me for?" –

Madame Gonzales well knew how to sound a note of hurt affection and wounded pride well known at the Academy of Dramatic Art. Monsieur Gunther begged her pardon, and made her sit down. But not a word more could he get out of her, until, at last, overcome by her master's insistence, she took her courage in both hands, and said:

"What you want at your age is a healthy, pretty young thing with sense enough not to ruin you physical powers: somebody who has not been picked out of the gutter, but a thoroughly nice, decent girl to whom you would not be ashamed to give your name."

"Oh! so that's it!"

"Yes, that's it. Marriage for a man of your sort is sheer lunacy so long as he is ruled by his appetites, and wants to taste of every dish. It would be no less lunacy if you were seventy and could look forward only to being an old gull. But you're at the time of life when a wise man eases off a bit, begins to go slow, and so arranges matters as to have his pleasure ready to hand under his own roof, all above-board and honourable, with the additional advantage, after he's past the age of forty, of costing next to nothing."

Mélanie stopped speaking. Her heart was thumping. She waited to hear what he would say. Monsieur Gunther got up, leaned against the mantelpiece, stared at the lady out of his greenish eyes, and said:

"I think we'd better put our cards on the table. Your reasoning is crystal-clear. I've no wish to be made a fool of, but what I don't see is what I'm going to get out of all this – except the pleasure of infuriating my children. Where you come in is obvious. Don't think I can't see what it's all leading up to, you sly old bitch!"

He gave a greasy chuckle. Madame Gonzales compressed her lips, and twisted round her fat finger the wedding-ring which Monsieur Gonzales had rather belatedly placed on it when almost at his last gasp.

"Yes, Bertie: I fully agree about cards on the table, and mine are there already. My dear, if we have understood one another so well and so long, hasn't the reason been that our interests are identical? They've never been more so than at this moment. Don't forget that your wife would be under my thumb. . . ."

"That's all very fine, but from what I can see, this Edith of yours is a great deal more interested in Edward than she is in me."

"What an old silly you are! Can't you see she's playing a game? You must agree that it's essential that your children's suspicions should be side-tracked, and that nothing must occur which might interfere with May's marriage?"

She did not wait for his answer but, with a finger to her lips, and an air of mystery, frisked to the door, leaving Bertie to his thoughts.

The large lady, armed with her parasol and her lorgnette, resumed her aimless wandering, apparently unoccupied, but actually obeying motives of which nobody but she knew the nature. It seemed, at first, that she had something to do in the pleached alley which abutted on the orchard. There she could sit, as in the abscurity of a stage-box. Between the trunks of the trees the orchard took on the appearance of a lighted scene. Madame Gonzales had good reason to point her lorgnette.

"Give me the ripest ones," May was saying to Claude who, perched on a ladder, was engaged in stripping a plum tree.

The face she turned up to him seemed to have been drained of colour by the heat. The glare made her blink her eyes. In her thick hair the sun was making little splashes of dark gold. Madame Gonzales could not catch what Claude was saying, but she heard May's little burst of young fresh laughter. Then

Claude began to come down the ladder. He stopped half way, and there was no longer any need for the girl to keep her face turned upward. She began to sort the plums. She threw away one which had a worm in it, and this Claude eagerly picked up and crushed against his teeth. May kept her eyes firmly fixed on his sandals. She was twisting the Indian bracelet on her sun-burned wrist. The blood was beating in the young man's temples. He clung to the rungs of the ladder, then, suddenly, his eyes saw nothing and he collapsed on to the grass. May uttered a faint cry and he opened his eyes. The adored face was bending above him, and its expression was one of amazed tenderness. Almost before their lips met May had scrambled to her feet. The faint touch of mouth on mouth, perhaps the smell of the young body, had sobered her. Claude watched her as she walked away towards the house. After remaining for a moment or two motionless, he, too, got up and left the Park. His rope-soled shoes moved silently along the road. The sun had ceased to shine. An overcast sky seemed to be weighing heavily upon the rounded outline of the hills.

May turned the key of her room door, entered, sat down on the *chaise-longue*, and remained there with her hands open. When the bell sounded she opened the window and called out that she would not be coming down to luncheon. Then, after closing the shutters, she once more relapsed, and lay following the movement of her thoughts. At one moment she saw herself as a criminal, dishonoured for ever: the next, she grew indignant at her own bourgeois cowardice. She felt ashamed, not because of the kiss he had given her, but because of the inferior social status of the man she loved. She got up, stretched, raised her rather square hands to her face, then squatted on the rug as, in their childhood, she and Edward had been used to do, with her hands clasped about her knees. 'If he were not just a country bailiff's son, if that kiss had been given me by one of Edward's friends, should I now be feeling so ashamed?' Again and again her mind came back to that same sore point. It was a mania with her, the result of her Huguenot training, always to judge the moral value of her actions, to feel her way back along the chain of motives and causes. She envied her Catholic friends who, as she thought, possessed a formula which allowed them precisely to classify their sins, a catalogue which would tell them which were mortal, which venial. Then, the puerile nature of that idea made her smile. 'But at least they have a director to turn to.' She had to admit to herself, however, that her pride would never let her confide in anybody to that extent. All the same, how lonely her religion made her! She remembered the death-agony of one of her father's sisters, and the amazement felt by one of her Catholic friends, because the clergyman could do nothing to help the dying woman.

She could hear on the floor below the sound of forks clinking against plates, the same sound which had reached her when, as a child, she had been in bed with measles, and had cried because she was not sitting with the others in the light of the great hanging lamp. She tried to pray. "Oh God, you have given me one guide only, my brother: but you have said that the blind cannot lead the blind. . . ." But the voice which once had calmed the stormy waters no longer sounded within her. 'How is it possible to believe that He resides in a tabernacle? If I believed that I should find some way of forcing Him in His house. . . . But Claude is one of those who do believe it.' Then her mind went back to the kiss she had received. Had it lasted long? Had the lips of the young man really touched her own, or only her chin? Had she felt joy, horror, or disgust? She remembered the warm, animal smell that had come from his open shirt . . . could she deny that she revelled in the memory? She cried for very shame. What had become of that inner certainty of hers that she would never be dominated by what the Pastor called the flesh? There had been a time when she had loved to think of herself as one of those sublime young women invented by some modern writers, had found happiness in ranking herself among those haughty virgins whom the craving for perfection, the willing acceptance of misfortune, the urgency of sacrifice, had attracted more than the happiness of a shared destiny. Many and many a time she had found pleasure in the sense of her own sublimity, though she had been worried by the thought of imposing renunciations upon herself, of immolating herself upon some unknown altar. "Whoso shall lose his life shall save it" – she had written that sacred text at the bottom of her secret notes, convinced that, like the heroines of her favourite novels, she was not at the mercy of base desires, would never know the intoxicating power of evil delights. . . . But now she saw herself only as a wretched, fleshey sister of the daughters of Eve, a slave to her body and her blood, a prisoner of the same instincts, the same appetites as those of the beasts of the field: a female.

Somebody was scratching at the door. Madame Gonzales appeared with a cup of soup. She had come to make sure that her "dear girl" was not unwell. May felt too contemptuous of her to pay the least attention to what she was saying. All the same, she could not help noticing that there was an extraordinary gleam in the eyes that showed under their blackened lashes, and, beneath the glib words, an air of insolence and triumph. She felt uneasy, and assured her visitor that she was better and wanted only to be let alone.

"Oh, I do so understand that, my dear girl!" answered Madame Gonzales unctuously, though she gave the lie to her words, by immediately settling down on the *chaise-longue*.

"You have never really understood me, May dear."

The girl uttered no protest. Motionless, and with an expressionless face, she fronted her enemy and waited.

Madame Gonzales continued: "In the days when you were my pupil I felt no surprise at your hostility: but now that you are grown up, don't you think you might look on me as a support, as a friend to whose advice you could listen?"

It gave her intense pleasure to see the colour mount in May's cheeks, and then drain away as the girl stammered out that she needed no support, and no advice.

"That's nothing but boasting, my dear. . . . You see, I do understand you so well. . . ."

"I am sorry that I cannot return the compliment," May answered in a toneless voice: "I can assure you, madame, that I am quite incapable of probing your many mysteries."

Madame Gonzales embarked extempore on a verbose and rambling dissertation. She knew, she said, a great deal about the young, and that from personal experience of youth: she could feel much sympathy for a young heart exposed to temptation – no very serious matter, provided one kept a firm hand always on the tiller.

"To what is all this leading, madame? I have got the most frightful headache, and want to get some rest."

Madame Gonzales showed no sign of wavering: "The situation has become too serious, dear child, and I am much too fond of you, even though you *may* sulk, to let a mere headache stand in the way of our discussing certain things. . . . You see, May, I know your secret."

"I have no secret, madame." Standing there, the girl tried to take refuge in bluster, but the hands she raised to her breast were trembling.

"It would be truer to say that you have one no longer," retorted the elder woman, and this time there sounded through her words a note of smug gratification. With shy archness, she added:

"I heard everything and saw everything that was going on, barely an hour ago, under a plum tree in a certain orchard."

"Then all I can say, madame, is that your eyes must have played you false."

With head thrown back, and a perfectly blank expression, May stood her ground for a few moments. But finally, Madame Gonzales' reticencies, sickly-sweet sympathy, and grubby insinuations got the better of her, and she collapsed in tears, like a little girl who can stand her ground no longer. Madame Gonzales looked at her as a sportsman might look at the pigeon quivering at his feet. She knew now, for certain, that sooner or later May would bear the name of Madame Castagnède, and that nothing would any longer stand in the way of Edith's becoming Madame Dupont-Gunther. Then she, made stronger by her double victory, would rule over Bertie far more surely than she had ever done in the days when they were lovers. She sat down at May's side and took the girl's moist hand between her own spatulate fingers. In a voice which had once more become smooth and wheedling, she begged the "dear child" to show that she had confidence in her, and protested that, provided she behaved sensibly, May need not doubt her discretion. There was a young man, she said, who for a very long time now had been her adoring slave, and was only too anxious to offer her an abiding happiness. . . .

These words echoed oddly in May's heart. Not one of them did she miss, though all the while the strangest thoughts were crowding in upon her mind. She felt within herself a complete absence of all will. It was as though her power of resistance had collapsed in ruins. The idea that the woman seated beside her was in possession of her secret – of *that* secret – made her

wish only to go somewhere very far away, to sink into utter
nothingness. Ah! if only there were someone to whom she
could cry in her despair! - but in the desert of her life all she
could see was Edward's uneasy smile, Edward's appraising and
emotionless gaze.

"After all, May, to make this marriage a reality, this marriage
in which your salvation lies, there is very little you are being
asked to do - the most that anyone expects is that you should
renounce the errors of Protestantism. On that point Madame
Castagnède will admit of no compromise. I know it is hard for
you to abandon what, till now, you have regarded as the truth,
but does not our holy religion offer you a greater certainty than
you can find in the Reformed Church?"

At any other time May would have laughed, and so cut short
Madame Gonzales' unexpected essay in apologetics. Actually,
however, while the fat lady was getting bogged down in
formulae, May was busy thinking about all that would precede
this marriage should she agree to it. So strongly was she
attracted by this so-called "sacrifice" that the marriage itself
appeared to her in the light of a mere accessory, while she
looked on her conversion as a form of renewal, as a fresh
beginning. Like a poor, injured gull, she saw the lighthouse.
For a moment she forgot Madame Gonzales, Marcel Castagnède, and even Claude, and remembered only Adeline Vala-
dier, once her dearest friend, and how, on their way home from
lessons, they had gone together into the cathedral more than
once. On those occasions May had remained standing, while
Adeline at her side had prostrated herself to shed the heavy load
of her charged heart.

In the darkened room she could hear Madame Gonzales'
words only as an indistinct murmuring. To herself she said: 'I
have nothing left: everything about me has been smashed to
atoms: every way out is closed to me except that single one by

taking which I can attain to freedom. Alone in the world, without a family to think of, I need trample on nobody in order to escape from the icy temple and enter into that warm darkness which will be starred with candles and filled with an infinite presence.'

"Can I rely on you to be sensible, dear child? Can I take a word of hope to your father?"

Madame Gonzales had risen to her feet. May gave her an affirmative nod, and said that she would not be coming down to dinner. When, at last, she was alone, she remained seated, with wide-open eyes, in the darkness. She was amazed to find how quickly time was passing. Impossible now to assuage the curiosity she had about her feelings. Suddenly, in imagination, she saw the Gonzales and her daughter gorging themselves on her miserable secret, could hear them laughing together at the idea that a single kiss given to a country lad should be capable of producing a conversion and a marriage. She wanted to cry aloud, to do herself some hurt. She would stand up to the whole world! She would marry Claude rather than seek a coward's comfort in Catholic idolatry! She fought tooth and nail to revive the dying flame of her pride. A sudden onset of desire brought her to her feet. She would seek refuge in her lover's arms. She spoke Claude's name aloud, and, even as she did so, felt that she was a criminal, and left her room, not knowing where to go. A shadowed form was waiting for her in the corridor. She recognized the voice of Madame Gonzales:

"Well, my dear, have you thought it all over?"

"This, madame, is something that concerns me alone."

Even while she uttered the insolent words, she remembered that this woman had "seen", and, even had she forgotten it, the – "what was that you said?" – which the other shot at her, would have been enough to bring her to heel. That was why she added, overcome by sudden cowardice:

"Don't think, madame, that I am not grateful for your advice."

At that moment, Madame Gonzales realized the full extent of her victory. "Everything will turn out for the best: just you leave it all to me, and give me the confidence I deserve, though up till now, you naughty thing, you have withheld it!"

She pressed the girl's rigid body to her breast, and then, discreet as ever, hurried away to set her other intrigues going.

May, walking like a blind woman, with hands outstretched, stopped at her brother's door. There was a gleam of light beneath it. At her knock, voices within fell silent. A chair was moved. She entered, and at first had difficulty in recognizing the faces turned towards her. Her brother was lying on the sofa with his knees drawn up. Edith was standing close beside him playing with a coral necklace, which is the poor girl's substitute for pearls.

"Am I disturbing you?" she asked stupidly.

"Of course you're not" Edward replied, rather self-consciously. "Would you like some tea? We were just having a snack and a chatter. The days pass very slowly here. . . ."

Edith offered May a plate of biscuits. Edward lay furtively observing his sister through a cloud of cigarette smoke. May thought that she could see in those familiar eyes a look of such distress that, for a moment, she forgot her own pain. Edith, on the other hand, was babbling away gaily. Her light-coloured dress seemed to be slipping off her shoulders. In a sudden mood of expansiveness she sought friendly words to keep May there. For the first time she felt that she was the richer of the two.

"Don't go yet: we'll have a little feast, just the three of us. Edward's biscuits, you know, are much nicer than the ones we get downstairs."

May repeated her former refusal, excused herself, and went out, closing the door behind her.

"Poor kid," said Edward. Edith shrugged:

"We did our best to make her welcome, didn't we? Your sister's always standing aside, always making an act of renunciation. Oh, it's easy enough to see that you are of the same blood, you two! You may bless your stars that you found me, ducky!"

She took Edward's face between her hands and drew it towards her lips with a look of adoration. Very gently, Edward freed himself, and said:

"Have we so much to congratulate ourselves about?"

Edith thought that she alone was the cause of his misgivings.

"I regret nothing: I have kept myself for you. Oh! don't run away with the idea that I am disinterested: disinterestedness is the virtue of cowards. I want to get something out of my life: from now on it shall be made of my love and for my love, with you and for you."

Edward looked away. Each word she spoke added a link to his chain. 'I am in my grave,' he said to himself, 'and somebody is piling stones upon it.'

Edith, whose precarious existence so far had taught her how to fight and how to scheme, failed to catch the note of his despair. Shared pleasure, and the sensuality of this weak and indolent young man, was quite enough to put a young girl off the scent, no matter how wide awake and shrewd she might be. Before meeting Edward, she had never given herself completely to anybody. She knew all about men when desire has them by the throat: she was used to being besieged, and excelled at twisting the male suppliant round her little finger. What was outside her experience was the sated, disappointed lover, eager only to make his escape.

She lit a cigarette and looked through a chink in the shutters, which were still closed, though the sun had already set.

"Ah! there's your father and my mother walking back together from the pleached alley. They seem very excited! Poor mother! she weaves her web with such very obvious threads, and is always quite sure that the victims will be caught! She's for ever telling me that I am not ambitious, yet, compared with mine, her ambition is a tawdry little affair! Because, you see, I want money, but I also want fame, and love – everything, in fact, that you and I will find together, darling, in your rue de Bellechasse flat, where we shall be before very long!"

It had been agreed between them that Edward should go away alone next day, and that Edith should join him, very soon, in Paris. He realized now, as he had never done previously, the full horror of the disaster which had befallen him. This woman was going to be established, perhaps for ever, in the refuge where he went to earth. How could he ever have suggested such a thing? Why had he not kept silent during their brief onsets of lust?

"How intensely we shall live, darling! Don't think for a moment that I shall want to cut you off from your friends. What we want is success, isn't it – which means that we shall have to be in with heaps of people, and even if it didn't, you share my passion for faces, for human beings. I am going to *force* you to become famous, dear lazybones!"

He asked her in what way he was to achieve fame.

"Dear heart, your painting, of course, how else? I've seen some perfectly charming things of yours. Didn't you have a very successful show, two years ago, at the Mannheim Galleries?"

Edward shrugged. For the past few months he had been aware of his lack of any real ability. He was the eternal amateur, and his pictures were no more than the reflection of what he admired in the work of others. Being interested only in himself, how should he not have been disgusted with what he produced, seeing that there was nothing of himself in it? His unbounded, and always vulnerable, pride could no longer endure the indifference, the contempt of genuine artists. But Edith kept harping on the the same string.

"It's perfectly true, you know. Firmin Pacaud says you have got a fine sense of colour . . . and that's not all. I've not been wasting *my* time . . . you won't laugh at me, will you? . . . the fact is, I've got a novel and a collection of verse all typed out. . . . Take that nasty look off your face, and don't say a thing until you've read them. . . . Oh, I knew you wouldn't approve, that's why I kept mum until I was sure of you. . . . Let me have my way, little man: I know so well what I want: you see, even if what I write doesn't amount to a row of beans, I've just got to go on. Can't you see that I just *must* be an authoress if I'm not to be merely a kept woman?"

Edward could not help admiring so great a knowledge of life. To himself he said: 'She's not the type to throw herself in the river if I leave her: she knows how to swim.' Edith continued to enlarge on the thrilling subject, without noticing Edward's air of gloom. He got up:

"The worst of the heat's been over for some time."

He pushed open the shutters. His silence did not worry her. She had succeeded in what she had set out to do. Without deliberately offering herself, she had surrendered to Edward so as to increase her hold on him. Fundamentally, she was incapable of resisting her instincts, and lived enslaved to her body. But what a tenacious determination could get, she had got, and was convinced now that she had rounded off her work to perfection. Nevertheless, she knew nothing of that race of clear-sighted men who are never blind to a trap, but let themselves be caught from sheer apathy, and put as good a face as possible on their defeat, yielding endlessly until a moment comes when they are just not there any longer, for the only courage they possess is that of flight, of shaking themselves free, and unloading the burden. Edward's blissful satisfaction in the pleasure of his body had deceived her to such an extent, that she felt no fear of his icy good manners. She would have dropped dead if, while she was nuzzling into her lover's shoulder, she could have read his secret thoughts: 'How she does love settling down to a good meal!'

IX

EDITH, lying with her eyes half closed, watched the morning sun touch with life the transparent roses of the cretonne curtains. Her mother came in. She was wearing no addition to her own scanty locks, and was wrapped in a pink dressing-gown with a pattern of storks on the wing. The remains of last night's make-up gave her face a dirty look, and there were pouches of brownish skin under her eyes.

"Edith, my pet, have you heard that Edward caught the ten o'clock train, and that he took a tidy lot of luggage with him? It looks as though we were rid of him for good."

Madame Gonzales had expected her daughter to show some sign of distress. All she saw was a smile – and it worried her.

"Did you know, you little humbug?" The girl offered no denial.

"You seem to be taking it all very philosophically, and, to be quite frank, I can't help thinking it's the best thing that could have happened. That young man was taking your mind off. It's the *father* we're interested in. You'll find it easier now to get a stranglehold on him. It's about time you and I got together. You haven't been much of a help so far, but I do think I have done everything possible in the circumstances. Your young man going off like this is really *most* fortunate."

Madame Gonzales broke off, somewhat concerned to see that Edith was still smiling. The girl took a cigarette from the bedside table, lay back on her pillows, and watched the smoke eddying above the bed. What, asked Madame Gonzales, jokingly, was going on in that cunning little brain?

"I can't help wishing you were crying, my dear: I'm not sure I like this way you have of saying nothing."

Edith, with an air of innocence, assured her mother that there was no reason why she should look particularly sad. Madame Gonzales retorted that, quite frankly, she didn't believe her. Not that there was any harm, she went on, in her having her bit of fun on the side, so long as it didn't take her mind off the main business.

"Tell me the truth, now: Edward didn't leave you entirely cold, did he?"

To this her daughter replied without the slightest show of emotion, that she would go further than that, and say that she was quite sure she was in love with him. Her mother, with a distinctly uneasy note in her voice, replied that, in that case, she must congratulate her for being able to get over so quickly a departure which meant the end of a dangerous flirtation.

Edith dropped her cigarette into the ashtray, and looked her mother straight in the eyes.

"It means nothing of the sort. In a week from now I shall be with Edward in Paris."

Yellow patches appeared suddenly on Madame Gonzales' forehead and sagging cheeks.

"You wouldn't be such a little fool!" Who, asked Edith, was to stop her?

"Do you really think, you little nincompoop, that I have

sacrificed my life to your future, that for years at the cost of my honour and my reputation, I have made things smooth for you, only to. . . ."

"Don't make such a noise, mother, please . . . it's not only extremely common, but very imprudent as well!"

The girl's studied coolness and ice-cold mockery now, as always, had the effect of putting Madame Gonzales off her stroke.

"Just you listen to me for a moment, mother. True, I am very much in love, but I happen to be ambitious as well, far more ambitious than you are, I want money, and a position in the world, quite as much as you want those things for me, but I also want something else, which old Gunther could never give me, happiness. Money would mean nothing to me if I didn't have love. I can have everything from the son that I could get from the father. He is rich, and he lives in Paris. The difference is that he can also give me what I consider to be essential."

"What a little fool you are! Can't you see that you've got the old man where we want him, that you've only to lift a finger and he'll marry you out of hand, whereas, with this gigolo of yours you'll be on the streets in next to no time!"

"I'm not so silly, nor so simple-minded as you seem to think. All this time that you've been barking up the wrong tree, and working away at the father, I've been concentrating on the son. It wasn't easy, I give you my word for that, but now I've got him tied up properly – I'm quite sure of that."

"Darling, you're twenty-eight, and you've no time to lose. Bertie's a cinch, the boy's far more doubtful. Listen, Edith" (her voice had suddenly become as soft and wheedling as a little girl's) ". . . listen to me. I know men, and I'm quite certain that this Edward of yours is not the type women can have any hold over. He's feminine – far more feminine than you are, far too much like a woman ever to love one. He's not got any use for women."

Edith giggled:

"I can only speak of what I know."

"I don't say that he mayn't have a liking for certain kinds of pleasure, and you, no doubt, think that you have hung a chain of habit round his neck which he won't easily shake off. . . . Oh, my poor child! I know that type! It's just when one thinks one's got them for keeps that they slip away. They'll let you get them all but to the very door of the Registry Office, but the day before the ceremony, they take the Orient Express, leaving a letter for you with twenty-five Louis."

"Your mention of so definite a sum leads me to suppose that something in your own past is clouding your judgment. . . . You and I are two different people. You're not capable of getting the better of Edward. . . ."

"Are *you* presuming to teach *me*?"

"In this matter, yes. . . . I admit that I shouldn't be nearly so successful as you in leading Bertie by the nose, but. . . ."

"Delicate negotiations are more in your way, is that what you mean? All right, my girl, just you wait and see, or, rather, don't wait. I still have hopes of making you see sense. After all, when the bird's in the bag, one doesn't just throw it away!"

Madame Gonzales knew her daughter too well ever really to believe that she could convince her. All the same, she'd still got a week in which to act. Monsieur Gunther was staying in Bordeaux over the coming Sunday. The game might be saved, even now.

That same morning May had no sooner gone downstairs than she set off through the vineyard and opened the rusty iron gate which gave on to a field-path which led to Viridis. A distant bell announced the conclusion of Mass. There was a mist over the fields which heralded a blazing afternoon. Blue butterflies were hovering about her feet, and lizards were sunning themselves on the stone walls, their hearts visibly beating. Her face was devoid of all expression, and gave no indication of her inner struggle. During the night hours she had reached a decision, and it had brought her peace of mind. Awakened at dawn, after a restless night, by the twittering of birds, she had heard – with a sense of wild indignation – the sounds of Edward's furtive departure, the noise of the car quietly moving off with its load of luggage. But she had got the better of her first feeling of distress, finding strength in a newborn determination to start a new life. Her brother had betrayed her! well, then, she would bother no more about him! Marcel Castagnède was no more to her than the outward and visible sign of this other life she was about to enter. She thought of the Church as a communion, as something that would make it possible for heart to speak to heart, as the final victory over her old enemy – loneliness. Another man would lead her along the firm, sure road clearly marked with a succession of definite observancies. No longer would she be a prey to uncertainty at every parting of the ways, at every cross-roads. The hideous stench with which her father, Edward, and the Gonzales mother and daughter had filled Lur, had begun to make her feel as though she were being poisoned, and the madness of the flesh which, for a moment, she had felt, weakened the dread she once had felt of the Castagnède house now lying open before her. As she walked she conjured up a vision of that life of domesticity in which she must at length resolve to let herself be buried.

These decent folk were sufficient unto themselves. For them the outer ring of cousins of cousins marked the limits of the known world. All that the race of Castagnède was capable of producing in the way of intelligence, sanctity, or heroism, worked itself out within the walls of an old house where generation had followed generation for hundreds of years. It was unthinkable that its daughters should marry outside the limits of the city, scarcely, indeed, outside the family circle, and never with anybody who did not live in the same street, or, at least in the same parish. The servants, though in receipt of very modest wages, could not get used to other situations, and those who were dismissed in a fit of temper from their unassuming paradise, could never rest contented until they had been taken back. Only very rarely was a stranger asked to dine, but when such an occasion did arise, the guest's memory of the food with which he had been served remained in his mind, as a source of wonder, for the remainder of his life. No outsider ever really took root in the Castagnède household. A distant relation from the Nord, who had once descended upon it, meaning to stay for a week, took to his heels the day following his arrival. Marcel, who was affiliated to the Bordeaux branch of the Neo-Monarchist party, and had been put in charge of an organized campaign of rowdyism and sabotage directed against a professor with pro-German sympathies, had once, on the occasion of a Congress, offered the hospitality of his mother's house to a number of eminent Parisians, all of whom were on the staff of the Party paper. Their particular form of wit, their jokes, their exaggerations, all of them completely incomprehensible to people living outside the metropolitan radius, that pride, common to all writers, which consists in settling the hash of a Lamartine or a Hugo with a phrase, exasperated the members of the Castagnède family, incapable as they were of "seeing the point" of an unfamiliar reference. They took everything quite literally, and were instinctively hostile to all talk that was not "up their street". May fully realized these things: she and Edward had often laughed over them together. The Castagnède clan had been for them, ever since childhood, a favourite target. But to-day she no longer felt like laughing. She *wanted* that ordered, that regulated, existence and, more than anything else, that climate of moral cleanliness and dignity. With people like that she would be protected from everything vile and base. In their eyes she need never fear to see the faintest flicker of malice.

The fact that she had not yet encountered on the path she was following the man she was hoping to meet, began to worry her. She had made up her mind to have a frank talk with Claude. 'After all, I do owe him that,' she had told herself in a burst of honesty. Then, suddenly, at a corner, close by a ruined mill, she saw him. He was walking with his eyes on the ground, and did not at once notice her. In his Sunday best he had far more the appearance of a "rustic" than in his working clothes. The jacket with its padded shoulders exaggerated his stockiness in the most ridiculous way. The sleeves were too short for him, and showed his wrists. His thick hands, with their almost complete absence of nails, looked monstrous. He was carrying a straw "boater" and sweating profusely. Under his unbuttoned waistcoat she could see a starched "dicky" fastened awry on his flannel shirt. The sun glinted on the oil with which he had tried to smarm down his rebellious shock of hair which was "frizzed" like a butcher-boy's.

Her first feelings were of shame and anger. To think that she could have allowed such an oaf to disturb her peace of mind! Then Claude looked up, and she saw in his eyes an expression of humble, frightened tenderness, the expression of a dog who has been stroked by mistake. . . . He did not approach her, but stood motionless in the middle of the path. At that moment May saw him as he was. The shoddy ready-made suit bought in Toulenne no longer deceived her. She recognized in him the healthy young athlete at the mercy of a boy's first passion. They were caught up, the two of them, in a sudden blaze, as when, in a forest fire, flames shoot from tree to tree. She, a young sapling, seeing before her this fine great oak in flames, trembled. She was terrified by the delicious emotion which thrilled her, which must, at all costs, be overcome. She dared not go towards him.

"I wanted to see you," she said at length. "I owe it to you to be frank, and you owe it to me to do me a service."

He stammered out that he was not worthy, and she, with a trace of condescension in her voice, continued:

"I like you, Claude, and I think you have kindly feelings towards me. Your education and intelligence entitle me to treat you as a friend, even as a brother, now that my real brother has abandoned me. . . ."

She stopped speaking, and Claude could find no word with which to break the silence. He stared at her. She went on:

"It is not only your understanding that makes me feel I can confide in you, but also your religion, your candid faith."

She must, somehow or other, risk an allusion to what had happened in the orchard. Quickly she made up her mind:

"You know what a lonely life I lead, Claude. Do, please, hold out to me a helping hand. You have seen me in the moments of my weakness. You know that I suffer from a morbid curiosity, that I have a craving for experience which I get from my brother, and that it sometimes leads me to do things which are not really worthy of me. . . . But I know now where my salvation lies, and you can be a great help to me. . . ."

Staggered by her words, not knowing what it was she was trying to say, Claude stood there, stock still, in the middle of the path, breathing heavily. She told him to put on his hat: she did not want the fierce sun to beat upon the back of his neck.

"At last I know what it is that is demanded of me. It is not just coincidence that a young man who, with my father's

consent, has asked for my hand in marriage, insists that first
of all I must become a Catholic. Don't you think, Claude, that
I am right in seeing in that a special intention towards me?"

"You're going to get married?" She pretended not to be
aware that he was suffering: she told him that there must be
comfort for him in the knowledge that he had done so much
to open the eyes of a little heretic. She expressed the hope that
he would crown his work by putting her in touch with
Monsieur Garros, or with the abbé Paulet, the parish priest
of Viridis. . . .

She was terrified that he might not answer. She could not
feel sure that he had even heard what she had been saying. He
had come close to her, and now gripped her wrist roughly.

"Who's the man? – young Castagnède, I suppose!"

She freed herself, and the droop of her mouth was so
expressive of disgust that Claude was appalled.

"I have said quite enough . . . probably too much, since it
seems I did not know you as well as I thought I did. . . ."

"F – forgive me! . . . forgive me!" he stammered.

But May, half running, had vanished behind the mill.
Claude did not follow her. At first he lay down in the ditch
which was dense with nettles and wild mint. Then, getting up,
he hurried through the vineyard, tearing himself on the
barbed wire, and never stopped until he reached Toulenne.
There he went into the first inn he saw, and sat down at
a table opposite the cowman, Abel. He called for white
wine.

May went to see her father next day in Bordeaux, and told
him of her decision. Bertie did his best not to seem too pleased.
No sooner had he been asked formally to give his consent than
he busied himself about the settlement. Marcel was to agree
that his wife's fortune should be left in the family business.

Monsieur Gunther, for his part, would raise no objection to his daughter's change of religion. The girl, who wished to avoid all further contact with the Gonzales couple, was to be left in Madame Castagnède's charge. The good lady introduced her to her confessor.

On Saturday, when Monsieur Gunther, with a beaming face and loaded with little presents, took his accustomed seat in the dining-room at Lur, Edith asked him to order the car for the follow morning. She would, she said, have a good deal of luggage. When he asked her, in the friendliest possible way, whether she expected to be absent for long:

"I am leaving Lur for good," she said, "a very dear friend of mine has invited me to her home in Seine-et-Oise, and I shall be there until the end of the holidays."

"This is all very unexpected, Mademoiselle: it would have been rather more considerate if you had communicated your intentions earlier."

"I told my mother, and this evening I have told you, of my plans, at the same time thanking you for all your kindness."

She spoke like a servant giving notice, and it was so obvious that she meant what she said that Madame Gonzales dared not raise her eyes from her plate and catch the eye of the choleric Monsieur Gunther. He, meanwhile, was addressing a question to her in a flattish voice:

"May I ask, madame, whether you were informed of this impending departure?"

She stammered stupidly that she had done everything possible to make Edith change her mind. This was tantamount to confessing that all their plans had been knocked sideways. But the storm did not burst at once. All three went through the gestures of eating, and the servant pressed forward with the ritual of the meal. Edith, alone, made a great display of having

nothing on her mind, and asked for a second helping of
chicken. She did not, however, stay for dessert, saying that
she had her packing to do. She pressed Monsieur Gunther's
hand and then, nonchalant as ever, walked to the door. Monsieur Gunther laid his napkin on the table, went into the drawing-
room, opened the window, and unfastened his collar. Finally,
he very quietly asked Madame Gonzales to explain what all
this business was about. The lady heaved a deep sigh. She
knew that she had lost the game, and that there was nothing
left for her now but to exact vengeance for twenty years of
humiliation.

"It amounts to this, my dear, that I have been proved wrong.
Disgust, in the case of my daughter, has been stronger than
pity."

"Disgust?"

"She has always (I have tried to keep it from you, but the
time has come to be frank) had a horror of all that is old and
outworn. She can love only the young. What she liked in you
she could love only in the person of your son. . . ."

"Get out! . . . get out, and take her with you! Between you
you have turned this house into a . . . brothel! For ten years
I've put up with you, and forced my daughter to endure the
ignominy of your presence here!"

A torrent of foul words followed. . . . They might have
been two tramps quarrelling in the gutter. But Madame
Gonzales continued to drink her coffee, with her little finger
raised. She watched Bertie's face becoming increasingly
purple. There was a very good chance, she thought, that he
might have a stroke, and the prospect was distinctly pleasing.
But he did nothing of the sort. What saved him, probably, was
finding relief for his blood-pressure by shaking his fist in the
lady's face, making a dash at her, snatching the cup from her
hand and smashing it to pieces on the floor, pushing her to the

door in spite of her clucking, and telling her to clear out at once. The two ladies took the 11.17 train from Toulenne.

At midnight Bertie was still in the drawing-room, brooding over an empty glass and a decanter of Armagnac. Now that the storm was over he was indulging in a solitary orgy. Satisfaction at having made a clean sweep left his nerves in a calmer state. That old spider of a Gonzales had spread a rather too obvious web this time! Still, the fact remained that he had been cheated of a succulent prey. The feel of Edith's body had given him a sense of ownership. . . . Bah! she'd have done nothing without a ring on her finger . . . and what a crude trap that sort of marriage would have been!

The realization that he was alone now in the house with two servants filled him with gloom. He was obsessed by memories of some of the more lurid films he had seen. He felt as though he were alone with a murderer in an isolated villa. A cat somewhere on the roof yowled savagely. To keep such dark thoughts at bay, Bertie set himself to recall all the things he had said to that old hag – and the memory was profoundly satisfying! She had put up scarcely any defence at all. He could not, however, help remembering one thing she had said. At the moment he had not given it a second thought, but it had stuck in his flesh like an arrow. He had suddenly become conscious of the smart. It had been about his daughter. She had said that anyhow it would be a relief not to have to go on looking after a hussy who let herself be messed about in corners by a country lout, adding that when he, Bertie, had compared his house to a brothel, he had spoken more truly than he knew. There suddenly came back into Monsieur Dupont-Gunther's mind the recollection of a letter in which Mélanie had warned him against Claude Favereau, who was in the habit of going bathing with Edward and May. . . . He shrugged his shoulders. Impossible to believe that the dreamy-eyed May, the little

Puritan who was prouder and more disdainful than a peacock, could have got herself involved with a clod like that! Mélanie had gone a bit far there! All the same, he could not help feeling a nagging anxiety, though it was driven from his mind almost at once by the picture of Edith in Edward's arms. A hideous jealousy took hold of him. He could have shouted his rage aloud. He decided not to go up to bed until the Armagnac was finished, and at once replenished his glass.

X

EDWARD DUPONT-GUNTHER *to* FIRMIN PACAUD
Paris, September, 19. .

I HAVE often told you before about the very special sense of happiness that comes over me when I get back from the country and slip into my old habits as into a dressing-gown with which I associate hours of work, smoke-dreams and reading. The sound of broken down old horses on wood paving drives away something of my blue funk. Looking at myself in the glass I see the almost visible disappearance of that strained expression which is the country's gift to me. Slowly it is replaced by the old familiar *me*. One by one the old tastes revive in me, the old ambitions, the old plans. . . . The old preoccupations of social life return with my resumption of town clothes and town interests. The telephone brings me the charming voices of those in whose company I can find amusement. There they all are, ready to entertain me. . . . I dream of possible sentimental attachments. . . . It doesn't last, of course.

My feverish desire to get down to work yields to a fixed belief that I am capable only of remembering what I have always been – a sham cubist to my fashionable friends, a smart amateur for such real artists as I know. I soon get sick of the telephone, and find it impossible to go on being amused for long by people in whom amusement is an insatiable appetite. My sentimental experiments lead to gloomy dead-ends. All I am left with is the last resort of solitude – the power of sitting by myself in a room which is the final bulwark against death. It is for those moments that I keep the sort of reading which opens metaphysical vistas to the mind. I am always careful to put away religion on a shelf, but like a pear to which one can have recourse when one is thirsty. Is it permissible, do you think, for a man who is defenceless against the temptation of death, altogether to ignore that ultimate reason for not hastening his end? Young Favereau's simple-minded faith (at bottom not so very simple-minded either) disturbs me a great deal less than that schoolboy heartiness of yours with its complete indifference to all that may underlie appearances. . . .

But this year's "return home" has been for me a time of mourning. Edith is here. She has made herself part of my day-to-day existence, though there is nothing about her of the wife showing a picture-book to her little boy under the lamp, nothing of the woman whose presence is solitude *minus* solitude's discomfort, of a woman whose regular breathing, I imagine, would stress the silence, but not disturb it. . . . Such households do exist. . . . Claude Favereau has told me so, and he knows me so little that he has actually advised me to acquire this simple but inaccessible bliss. Edith is very different. Edith is a mistress, with a mistress's power to lord it over my time, my books, my body. My life has become for her a game of chess, and she is busy organizing my future in accordance with her own very undistinguished standards. She sits there weaving her web, wrapping me round in its sticky threads, while I play 'possum, calming her fears and confident in my power suddenly to disappear, and quite certain that I wear upon my finger the ring of invisibility. Dear Pacaud, I know that you always side with the woman in these situations, but wait a bit before you let your softer feelings get the better of you. It may well be that she will take the initiative in this matter of flight. Such abilities as she has fit her admirably for life in Paris. Already she does not really need me. She will go far – that, certainly, is the opinion of her dear mother, who quite shamelessly descended upon us after the Lur drama, and plans to set up as a Beauty Specialist in the rue Gaudot-de-Mauroy. I consented to receive the good lady once, and once only. She is perfectly capable, if it comes to that, of cutting herself adrift from her daughter, if, by so doing, she can further her plans. But I am a distinct source of worry to the old campaigner. She doesn't trust me. No matter what I say, she knows instinctively that there's no doing anything with a man of my sort. I rely on her to help me get rid of Edith without too much of a scene. If you'd like to have a peep at this farce, come along some time about mid-January. By that time Edith will have found the flat of her dreams, and you and I will be able to sit far into the night smoking and drinking. It will be quite like old times. I shall have to sell some more of my Suez to meet the costs of this new establishment . . . what a bore!

Yours
Edward.

P.S. What's the news of May, her conversion, and this ridiculous marriage? She doesn't answer my letters. I know how she can harbour a grudge, and can only suppose that from now on she'll consider me in the light of an enemy – but not, as she has persuaded herself, because I left her in the lurch. It is *she*, really, who has betrayed *me*, and gone over to the camp of those who want to live.

Letter from FIRMIN PACAUD *to* EDWARD DUPONT-GUNTHER
(fragment)

. . . I'm not much bothered about whether or no Edith gets clear of you. I'm quite easy in my mind about the temporary set-up, so far as you are concerned, because I know how curiously unsuited you are for passion with a big P. But what does make me feel worried is this determination of yours to break down all your defences, and to loosen every bond that holds you to life. I keep telling myself that you talk far too much about death ever to seek it deliberately: but that doesn't alter the fact that I should be more comfortable in my mind if I knew that you had developed some ambition, some mania – perhaps, even, some vice, anything, in fact, that would fill your days. Shut yourself up in your studio, choose a master, and work. Any wretched dauber can convince you that you have no talent: there is something in you that always meets those who make sly and cunning attempts to discourage you, half way. Dear Edward, you like to think that you have got beyond caring what people say, but, actually, the most idiotic judgment can upset you! Well, then, if you can't work, and are, as you insist, incurably incapable of love, do at least cultivate that taste of yours for preferring the thrill of studying others to doing anything yourself. There was a time when you loved Paris parties. You often used to tell me of the conversations you had had with certain folk, conversations which, according to you, revealed abysses from which the most audacious of novelists would recoil. Is that sort of curiosity dead in you? I feel so worried about you, that I'd be only too glad to know you'd found some way of amusing yourself – no matter how squalid or ridiculous it might be.

. . . I gather that our May has taken to the water of her new pond far more easily than one would ever have thought possible. This piece of information comes to me from your father. I am not myself on visiting terms with the Castagnède gang. May might be in a convent for all anybody sees of her. Not a day passes but what she visits her two sisters-in-law to be, whose ideal in life is to be perpetually in a state of pregnancy or nursing motherhood. She is learning all about child-care. She goes every morning to early Mass. It's all very odd. She has broken away from your influence with so passionate a determination that I can't help feeling something is going on of which we know nothing. Do you remember how moonstruck she looked that evening at Lur when the Castagnède faction came to dinner? Haven't you heard anything? Perhaps my affection for her has led me into being a bit indiscreet. Although my reputation as a gay dog did do me a good deal of damage with your sister, there were times when she would listen to me, and, in your absence, tell me a little about herself. If only I had been ten years younger! . . . She has rushed away to hide in the darkness of a world of mysteries, and is getting drunk on the opium of Christianity. . . . Perhaps the effect of all this will be to produce a little sister of that Jacqueline Pascal, who always refused to set a limit to purity and perfection, whom you taught me to love. But there's always fat Marcel to reckon with. Will he know how to handle her? So far his role has been confined to assisting at the process of conversion. All the same, he is a young man, and he's got a trump card up his sleeve, though what the effect of *that* will be we shan't know until after the ceremony. Your father's hoping that it won't be long delayed, but old mother Castagnède insists that her future daughter-in-law shall first be thoroughly instructed in the

Christian mystifications. I don't myself think that the marriage will come off before the Spring.

Your father is losing weight, a bad sign in men of our age. The departure of the Gonzales was a blow to him. I am told that he has broken with Rosa Subra – I've certainly never known him to be so long without a woman of some kind. He drops in quite often of an evening to see me. It's that 1853 Armagnac of mine that's the attraction. I enjoy seeing him: he doesn't bore me in the least. You see, my dear boy, we share so many of the same tastes – to say nothing of memories! Business isn't too bad, I chose just the right moment to get in the whole of my Entre-Deux-Mers crop. There's been hail in the Aude since we finished. But you'll be wishing me at the devil. . . . Don't you think you might unearth as part of your bourgeois inheritance a taste for business and money? It wouldn't, you know, necessarily mean an end to intellectual curiosity. I'm pretty good proof of that. . . .

Letter from EDWARD DUPONT-GUNTHER *to* FIRMIN PACAUD
(fragment)

Paris, March, 19..

. . . Solitude has been given back to me at last, and if I didn't still find hair-pins in my ash-tray and the clinging smell of Chypre on the cushions, above all, if Edith didn't sometimes pay me a surprise visit and plump herself on my knee in that thoughtless way that women have, because they are apparently of the opinion that love makes them light, I could almost believe that I was back in the happy old days when I could suffer undisturbed.

It took us three weeks to find the flat. Edith would not even consider looking outside the 16th arrondissement. We penetrated into endless cream-coloured entrance halls of the bogus-luxury type, and entrusted ourselves to the mercies of so many different kinds of lift, that I suggested writing a comparative study of Pifre and Samain. It never occurred to me that she could find any reason for hesitating between identical apartments: drawing-room all doors, no pannelling, and opening through vast sheets of glass on to minute vestibules: coloured glass in the dining-room windows of precisely the same pattern as those on the staircase, and the same enamelled corridor leading to the same bedrooms. At long last, however, she signed a lease, and though it meant my having to sell a lot more Suez, it had the enormous advantage of letting me have some sort of life of my own. There was nothing more to do except to make the rounds of the antique dealers, since Edith wouldn't hear of anything but "old stuff", because, according to her, the value "always goes up". She's as strong as a horse, and thinks nothing of turning armchairs upside down in search of "signatures". In the meantime, *Vierge Folle* by Edith Gonzales, with a clever little preface by Edward Dupont-Gunther, has appeared. Being a painter, I am credited by the Great World with having some small talent as a writer. The book has been a success: have you read it? It's a morbid affair, all very smart, with a fashionable touch of the lesbian. A careful observer could easily distinguish, in superimposed layers, everything that Edith has ever read, beginning with the honest-to-god edifying little books (dating from the time when she was a Child of Mary) and going on to the others (which belong to the days of her earliest temptations, her first fall from virtue, and all her various sex experiments . . .).

The really important thing is that I was able to persuade Madame Tziegel and the Comtesse de La Borde, that they had "discovered" Edith. This discovery has made a great deal of noise in our little set. Edith who, in the Castagnède house would have been given her meals apart, is here treated as a

Muse for the Modish. The little minx has mastered to perfection
the art of always being at home, never to shriek with laughter
when a duchess rings the bell, never to keep people at a distance
when she knows that they are only too anxious to come
running. In addition, she has learned how to flatter the literary
gentlemen, how to burn precisely the type of incense they most
want to snuff up. It is a difficult art, but the happy woman
who can make it her own is assured of what is usually known as
a "salon". "I really have to keep open house!" sighs Edith.

I was perfectly right in my prediction that she might leave
me before I left her. She began the softening up process long
before she really believed that I was sick of her. All the same,
she depends upon me. I have introduced her widely: I am a
useful stop-gap at dinner-parties, I pay the bills. I suppose you're
surprised that I should be so keen on keeping somebody who
bores me? My dear chap, I'm all impatience to start off in
response to one of her invitations. I am the first to arrive, the
last to leave. It's not a question of love, but simply because I'm
bored, lonely, and – to make a clean breast of it – as frightened
as a sick child. . . . Sometimes, when we've been dining together, I beg her not to hurry away, so terrifying, at certain
times, is my dear mistress solitude. Edith has good reason to
think that she is necessary to me. Old mother Gonzales, who
goes round every morning to massage her, pours oil on the
flames of her matrimonial ambitions. . . . I'm living in dread
of an ultimatum.

You advise me to read. You, too, as a schoolboy, were told
"there's no sorrow which fifteen minutes with a book won't
cure." But, my dear fellow, you don't know how tedious I find
every description of printed matter! When I see in the younger
types of periodical that men of my age once took sides for or
against Madame Bovary, and were terribly concerned over the
question of whether Moréas had genius or not, I feel deeply

humiliated, having to confess to myself that, since the days when I read Jules Verne with my fingers stuck in my ears, no book has ever managed to keep me from thinking about myself. Oh! if only I could see myself as the subject of a book, if only I could read myself as one reads a novel! That sort of mania has been the salvation of many.

Sometimes I think about Lur, the shade in the pleached alley, and about Claude's heart. . . . But as the result of a pretended sacrilegious pact which, one evening when I was in a particularly savage frame of mind, I suggested, I have lost him for ever. By alienating his affection, I have torn up my last card. . . . How, I wonder, can I explain that to you. . . .

XI

CLAUDE burrowed into the winter which, that year, was so rainy that the young man spent whole days at a time reading in the kitchen. He took down books from the shelves just as they came, and not as the result of deliberate choice, wandering about in the icy gloom of the library, carrying them to the light and spelling out their titles, as a diver might uncover, under the sun's glare, an orient pearl which he had fished up from the ocean depths. Seated in the chimney corner he gave himself up to his reading, while his father slumped in a chair with a bottle before him, and snored himself, now and again, into a state of wakefulness, while his mother, by the window, so as to get what remained of the daylight, sat endlessly darning. Sometimes, flinging a sack over his head, and putting on his clogs, he plunged, no matter how bad the weather, into the thick fog of damp and mist, and set off at random up the hill, along the flooded path between the twisted willows. Flocks of birds lumbered across the sky, alighted all together on the bare fields, and, then, the world became for Claude that place of appearances of which he had read in his philosophy textbook. There was nothing in the scene to distract him, nothing to keep him from seeing May wandering from hill to hill. In the dismal drench of that wet season he would suddenly see in imagination the narrow path in the midday sun, and the young girl standing there motionless, throwing a round patch of shadow. Then he would shake his head and shut his eyes in an effort to rid himself of the grubby, melancholy, obsession. Winter's isolation, the lack of anything to do, condemned him to be the slave of those gloomy, sensual broodings from which he could liberate himself only during the seasons when labour was heavy on the farm. He no longer thought with respect of the arrogant young creature whose face had once, for a moment, leaned near to his – the swimming eyes, the mingled breath, the hands pressed each to each! . . . Later, under the lamp, in his corner by the fire, while Favereau snored and the ceaseless rain closed in upon the house, the barns, the distant countryside, and, later still, in his iron bed, the bed of his childhood, with the dim glimmer of the darkness filtering through the uncurtained window panes, he was nothing more than the passive prey of his desires.

He came in one evening with a pain in his side and a high fever. His mother applied a compress of that "red water" of which she had the secret. "It'll purge him," she said, and, in spite of her anxiety did not at once call in the doctor who charged three francs for a visit: besides, Claude had had just such an attack the year he had made his First Communion. Favereau treated him as a malingerer who wanted to put off going back to work. When, at last, the doctor was summoned, he diagnosed a double pleurisy. Claude let himself sink into the depths of his illness with a sense of deliverance. Lying with his face to the wall, he muttered unceasingly, scraps of verse, vague phrases, impossible stories, pretending not to hear the questions put to him by his mother. The stains on the white-washed walls fell into designs which he took apart and recomposed as though they had been clouds. The ticking of the clock, the cries of birds, were not sufficient to give him the assurance that he was still alive. In the country, when the earth begins to demand man's tireless efforts, the sick know a solitude which nothing and no one can disturb. This complete abandonment brought to Claude a feeling of delight. He watched the slow fading of the daylight, the oncoming of the dusk, the silent fall of night, watching the scarcely perceptible degrees by which these changes came about. He suffered no pain, and was unaware of hunger. He realized how easy it is to become detached from everything. When the doctor came to see him, he exaggerated his weakness so as not to have to answer more questions than were absolutely necessary. As he grew stronger the first soft-boiled egg reminded him of the ailments of his childhood.

One day he was sitting on a bench under the trellized vine, in the March sunshine. Hens were scratching round his feet. The scene was still wintry, but a fragrance in the breeze, a certain quality in the light, seemed to announce that the moment of change was not far off. Between the withered leaves he could see a yellow flower all wet with dew. The artless blossoming of the fruit-trees had begun. The sun was already causing the sap to rise. Tremblingly it mounted, swelled at the tips of the black branches, filled the sticky buds.

The postman, without dismounting from his bicycle, threw down a newspaper and a letter addressed to Maria Favereau, whose spectacles were sliding down her hen-like beak. She said:

"Mercy me! the young people are going to spend the first night of their honeymoon here!"

"What young people?"

Didn't Claude know that Miss May was getting married to the Castagnède boy in the late Spring? There was going to be a great dinner at Lur for the estate workers. There'd be only just time to put the house to rights! Favereau laughed coarsely, and said they'd better choose pretty strong sheets. Claude got up, supported himself with his hands against the wall, and tried to recover the blessed torpor of his weeks of sickness. It was only in the middle of the night that he became fully awake, and felt the onset of his pain. The fact that he was overcome by a sense of gloomy happiness at the idea of seeing May again, amazed him. Yes, he would see her, even though another would hold her in his arms. He would see her wandering under the pleached alley in the morning light, pale and despairing. He would spy out upon her face the marks of horror and disgust. For this overgrown boy, so ardent and so sensual, the mysteries of the flesh were still sin and the withering away of innocence. With an animal sensuality he combined an agonizing longing for purity. The smallest falls from grace, the memory of which would serve only to amuse others, filled him with a mounting remorse. He remembered each occasion and its heinous details. He could make no allowance for the troubles of his adolescence, for the agony of his awaking senses, but recalled each accompanying thought and each desire. Not for a moment did he doubt that the realities of marriage would seem abominable to her whom he had seen turning away her mouth under his passionate breathing. The former seminarist could attribute to the sacrament no purifying influence. To him it had seemed the least of two evils in the case of Edward, who was incapable of leading a pure life, and, for that reason, he had advised his young master to settle down in marriage. In his heart of hearts he was only too ready to agree with Pascal's condemnation even of Christian marriage, when he defined it as "the most dangerous and the basest of all the states of Christian living, vile in itself and prejudicial in the eyes of God." He had never envisaged for himself the joys of wedded bliss, so sure was he that he could never set limits to the delights of the flesh. To this hot-blooded young man it seemed easier to abstain altogether than to regulate the intoxication of the senses. He did not doubt for a moment that once married, he would have abandoned himself to a frenzy of desire, and been incapable of keeping his bodily appetites within bounds. He was quite certain, therefore, that May, on the morrow of her initiation, would seek desperately – though God knew where! – a refuge, being unable to find consolation for her lost innocence.

Health flowed back into him. His mother wanted him to help her with the work of getting the house ready. He knew what ought to be done, she said, "as though he were a real gentleman". One April day, after the midday meal, he made his way through the front door. The fragrance of the past summer still hung about the house. He touched with his hands the sun-hat which was in its usual place, the very hat May had been wearing when he saw the gleam of her teeth and the parting of her lips in a defeated smile. In the drawing-room, where Maria was moving the furniture, he opened the piano. His fingers moved over the keys from which May had drawn for him so devastating a magic. Maria wiped the glass over the mantel-piece with a damp rag. Claude stared at himself in it. Illness had left him looking more vigorous, bigger, than ever. In his almost baby face the eyes seemed smaller than they had done before he took to his bed. So broad had his chest become that he could no longer button his shirt across it. He began to polish the floor, to wax the wooden panels of the old presses. With his sleeves rolled up, he washed the windows and moved the heavier objects. That evening, no sooner had he finished dinner, than he flung himself upon his bed and fell into a dreamless sleep.

He developed a liking for his new work. One day his mother called down to him from the top of the stairs. Her lips were parted in an almost ribald grin, revealing her two solitary teeth. It was a question of getting the bridal chamber ready, of making up a double bed. Claude, like a wounded man, pressed on his hurt in spite of himself. He could not stop from making it ache again, and made a point of arranging the furniture with his own hands. 'It is here,' he said to himself, 'that her husband will fill her with a feeling of such disgust that only in the memory of my shy and religious love will she find comfort.' He longed now for the consummation to be achieved and done with.

At about the same time, May, one evening made an entry in her private diary.

"This morning: Communion, my first. Father had warned me, and I felt quite certain that I should be disappointed. He had said that at first I should find only emptiness and silence, that I mustn't expect to feel anything. Was it because I had been expecting coldness that I found warmth, joy, calmness and peace? My attitude was one of complete surrender. I could not pray. 'He' was there, no longer inaccessible as in the days when I was a heretic, but present – in the body. I summoned up, one by one, all the dear faces of the living and the dead, that they might be participants in the grace which had visited me. It was the ordinary Low Mass, without singing, without any external stimulous to the emotions. What I felt, therefore, can have come only from inside me, from the sense of His presence. On my way home, everything seemed to produce in me a feeling of astonishment – the Spring greenery, the crowd, the little cars standing by the pavement. I was certain that from now on I had a refuge from life, that I should never again be alone. Breakfast . . . an indescribable look of nobility and purity on my future mother's old face, about which I had so often laughed in the days of my foolishness. I begged her to take me with her when she visited her poor. Had a sense of guilt because I had wanted her to admire me. Her especial liking for the old woman with cancer. I am sure it was because of the smell that she stayed longer than she need have done beside that bed. When I felt myself going pale, she got up. The way she kissed the cheek of the little girl with spots all over her neck. . . . I used to make fun of her, but now she arouses in me feelings of the deepest respect. . . . Rather worried in the afternoon. Had I been sufficiently precise when describing the evil thoughts which obsess me? On the other hand, if I were in a state of mortal sin, should I be feeling so happy? Had a talk with Father, who dissipated that particular cloud. I told him how ashamed I felt at taking everything and giving nothing, at not being conscious of suffering. My first feeling about this marriage was that it must be regarded as an act of expiation, but when I am with Marcel I have no sense of hostility. Complicated people, sick people, have wounded me too deeply. What pain their dryness of heart has caused me! It is only with difficulty that I keep myself from actually hating that brother of mine whom I once loved so dearly. I am looking forward to a life of security and peace with a perfectly simple man in whom there are no unplumbed depths, no deep gulfs. Father told me that what, first and foremost, was required of me was to accept willingly the common destiny of women. I must stifle all immoderate longings in matters spiritual, and fight against the attraction that I used to find in the idea of extravagant sacrifice. The wish to appear different is wrong: so is Huguenot pride in certain types of renunciation. I must not try to get ahead of grace, but to follow where it leads. That is my director's advice. No penance other than what is authorized by him. A regulated, not an impulsive charity."

On another occasion she wrote:

"The betrothal feast. I longed to be put to the test – and I have been, so cruelly that I can find a refuge only at Thy feet, Oh Lord! In the drawing-room after dinner, Firmin Pacaud, with his usual tactlessness, asked where we were going to spend the wedding night. Marcel replied that we had not yet made any plans, but that what he would like best would be to spend it at Lur. Without really thinking what I was saying, I burst out – 'Oh no! anywhere rather than Lur!' I felt that I was blushing violently. Father missed nothing of all this, but looked at me with those piercing eyes of his. Perhaps he *knows*. What a fool I am! How could I think for a moment that the Gonzales couple, when they left the house, would deprive themselves of so delectable a vengeance! I had sufficient control of myself to add, in a low voice, that, all things considered, the horror I felt at the thought of Lur was quite irrational, because those who once hated me had gone from it, never to return. Father heaved a sigh of relief. Firmin Pacaud was looking at me very intently. So I am going to spend my wedding night in the very place where I once gave way to weakness and torment of heart. . . . God send that he of whom I am thinking will decide to remain out of sight. . . . I expect he will suffer – that is if he hasn't forgotten all about me. But he is not one of the forgetting kind: he's the praying kind. . . .

" . . . A feeling of certainty that it is through him that grace has visited me. It makes no difference that when I knew him he was a prey to temptation, a slave to his own youth. I am sure that he was the bearer of infinitely more than himself. Obsessed by tormenting desires, subdued by the urgencies of flesh and blood, he believed that he could communicate something of his flame to me, and, all unknowing, gave me God. Grace spread from the mere fact of his being there, as light spreads from a lamp. It welled from his body's craving, and I received it."

XII

WHEN Claude woke up on the morning of the twelfth of May, the slip of a pale moon was melting into a fresh, unsullied blue which set him dreaming of the world's first age. He thought that he could hear for the first time since Winter ended the "earliest pipe of new-awakened birds". He felt that it was he who was the young bridegroom standing on the threshold of his bridal morn with a flurry about him of startled wings. He surrendered to the charm of this false happiness, and cherished in his heart the lying thought that it was he, the well-beloved, whom this new world was greeting. Through the litter of the room he tried to mark the very spot from where, when night fell, she would come to him, and it was only then that he could pluck up courage enough to tell himself that another would be seated at her side. He dressed in haste and went down into the kitchen where Maria was watching a woman from the village lighting the fire, though he scarcely heard her expression of relief that it was the cook from the *Cheval blanc* who would be in charge of the feast.

"Hard work and me sticks so close that I don't rightly know what to do with m'self," she said.

There would be eighteen in the great barn to eat and drink in honour of the young mistress. There had been four joints ordered, six fowls, and a great pie. Wine would flow like water.

"See that there's flowers in all the rooms: that something you can do. Our young lady always liked the way you done the vases."

Claude went out to the orchard. The high grass soaked the ends of his blue cotton trousers. Butterflies were fluttering in the mounting sun. He chose a plum-tree to lean his head against, and for him it was the tree of the knowledge of good and evil. He made no effort to prevent the uprush of desire, the sinful cravings of his flesh. As he conjured up a picture of May, all sweet and willing surrender, filthy words remembered from his army days swarmed back into his mind. 'She'll have been through the hoop,' he thought.

The trestle table used at the grape harvest had been set up in the barn. In the kitchen doorway Favereau was enumerating with gusto to the guests all the dishes that were to do honour to the day. He was especially eloquent on the subject of the wine. There would be twelve bottles of the 1906.

"No better year since '93."

The men agreed with him. Tirelessly, in patois, they exchanged liturgical phrases about vintages. There was no argument, for all were of the same opinion. On the dogma of fine growths there was complete unanimity.

When Claude appeared the girls nudged each other with much giggling and clucking. His starched collar was choking him. His jacket was so tight across his shoulders that it was nearly splitting. As soon as the steaming tureens were set upon the table, the men "stripped for action". Claude sat next to

Fourtille, and, no sooner had he taken his place, than he felt the pressure of her knee against his. In next to no time he had filled and emptied his glass more than once. The smell of human bodies began to mingle with that of the food. Maria was glad to see Claude laughing, drinking, and shouting with the others: 'If he don't want to be a fine gentleman, 'tis better he should be like one of us.' With a tolerant and sympathetic eye she saw Fourtille leaning an amorous cheek against his shoulder.

"My cock is loose – look out for the hens!" she cried in patois. The remark was greeted with loud laughter. By this time Abel was too drunk to heed the warning. Claude had reached that first stage of drunkenness when a man thinks himself master of his fate, and, with a lucid eye can take the measure of his wretchedness. He ate slowly, like an ox, like all the others round the table for whom the pleasure of this feast was the best things life had to offer. He surrendered to the dizziness of this fall into the abyss of animal sensations. Fourtille's body was burning hot to his touch. At this moment of final and utter defeat he would summon satiety to his aid, which would be the next best thing to death, would plunge into a gratification where the ghost of the lost girl could not pursue him. Favereau, purple in the face, and with bloodshot eyes, got up and went out. Another followed suit. Fowls were pecking round the table. In the brief moments of silence the sharpening of scythes could be heard from distant fields, the crowing of cocks, and the barking of dogs. Claude emptied his glass again. His very misery kept complete intoxication at bay. The memory of the flowers that he had plucked that morning and had not yet had time to arrange, gave him an excuse for leaving the company.

On the billiard-table mounds of lilac were giving off a sweet smell. He began to fill the vases. One of them was of reddish earthenware, and it came back to him how much May had admired the effect of the brilliant blue against it. He put some early roses with the lilac, and decided that the bouquet would look well on the bedroom mantelpiece. Accordingly, he went upstairs and opened the door. The sheets made a pure, unbroken line in the gloom. The fragrance of lavendar and fennel hung about them.

Claude sat down. He was no longer suffering, and comforted his heavy heart by conjuring up a fiction which, since his convalescence, he had endlessly repeated. He saw, in imagination, the girl's violent reaction, saw her seeking in the arms of the country lad whom once she had loved, refuge, comfort, and forgetfulness. His lips formed the words that he would speak to her, burning words, but chaste and innocent of all offence. He would touch with his mouth the tired eyes with their salty taste of tears. Might not hours, days, weeks, months, years slip by without a loosening of that embrace: might not the two lovers, thus merged, thus bound, escape into eternity?

He got to his feet at last, and, in the half light, set about decorating the house with lilac. The blossoms were already wilting. No need for him this evening to put in an appearance at supper. Favereau would be sleeping off the effects of the wine he had drunk, and Maria would be getting dinner for the young people. On his way through the dining-room he stopped for a moment and stared at the two places laid opposite one another. Then he went out. The level light touched the young green of the grass, and, away in the distance, made the poplars cast long shadows. The three notes of a nightingale sounded distinct and separate as drops of water. Coupled cockchafers were falling from the leafy chestnuts. It was the season of the year when Venus shows large and wonderful in the still sunlit sky.

He leaned on the terrace balustrade. Along the grey ribbon of the road already plunged in darkness, two dazzling lights were coming towards him, growing in size as they drew nearer. The roof of foliage above the avenue gleamed briefly as though caught in the glare of a Bengal Light. He could hear Maria's voice above the purring of the car's engine. There was a burst of laughter, the sound of a door being shut, and then, once more, the croak of frogs answering one another. From all the countryside there rose that nocturnal trilling which is the forerunner of the great heats.

Claude slept as soundly as a child, and got up early because he had not finished weeding the paths. Would she dare show her tired face in the morning light? Would she be able to conceal the ravages of horror and dazed stupefaction? – or would the signs of her disgust be visible for all to see? Ah! with what delight would Claude receive their message!

A "good-morning, my man" made him turn his head. He saw Marcel Castagnède, who was still wearing his pyjamas. His healthy young cheeks, touched by the morning freshness, were glowing. His grey eyes looked out, small and glinting, between puffy lids.

"Lend me a pair of shears: I want her to have roses by her when she wakes."

He moved away, despoiling the rose bushes as he went.

"The fool has seen nothing, understood nothing," said Claude to himself. "He is incapable even of noticing that she is in a state of mental agony."

It seemed to him that a heavier silence hung over Lur than when the house had been empty. Men and wind had built about its walls a soundless universe. He gazed at the windows, especially at two on the first floor, which had their shutters ajar. Smoke was rising and drifting away above the kitchen roof. Not once all afternoon did the young pair show themselves in the garden. Claude let his imagination play about the gloomy drama which must, even now, be going forward in the shadowed room. The silent despair of the woman, he thought, was making one with his own, as a river makes one with the sea into which it flows, as once the music of *l'Invitation au Voyage* had washed over his heart like a storm. Had it ever since then ceased, for a single moment, to dash him to pieces in vast ocean depths? No doubt May was waiting for darkness before showing her tear-stained face. In utter loneliness she would take upon her cheeks the soft night breeze that it might wipe away the scars of kisses and wipe her clean of all defilement. The prospect filled him with delight. He gave himself to the joy of that despair in one whom he loved more than anything in the whole world. Without the sense of that despair he could live no longer. The savage selfishness of passion made him ugly. Bestial and cruel, he waited for the moment when, hidden among the bushes like some rustic god burning with desire, he could feast his eyes on the spectacle of a young and outraged body seeking concealment, eager for flight, weeping because for ever now it must be condemned to daily violence and the defilement which each night would bring.

The light began to fade. A startled cuckoo took wing suddenly from the pleached alley, its double note growing fainter as it flew towards Les Landes. A swarm of cockchafers began to drone once more about the leaves which they had eaten into shreds. Favereau passed by on his way to spray the vines. There were blue stains on his smock. Caubet and Lauret came home, the bones showing through their skins because when work was hard they went hungry. Their flanks were heaving like those of bulls in the arena in the final moment before collapse. Claude heard the gate creak, and plunged into the shelter of a shrub. There, leaning against an oak, he waited. At first he saw nothing, though he recognized Marcel's voice, the sound of which was broken now and again by bursts of fresh young laughter. Claude convinced himself that the laughter sounded false, told himself that he could hear in it the message of a desperate irony. But already he was beginning to be tormented by doubt. He held his breath. The young people turned into a path which ran parallel with the pleached alley. They turned a corner, and he could see them clearly. They were not arm in arm, but hand in hand like children who have been told to run away and play in the garden, and to be good.

"There's no one here," said May. "The worst of this place is that the country people are always on one's back."

Claude remembered that he had heard the same insolent phrase on the lips of Madame Gonzales. The couple moved towards the terrace. Claude could see them standing side by side. A light breeze was playing in the young woman's scarf. She leaned her head until it rested on the man's shoulder. Even now Claude tried not to understand. He scraped his forehead against the bark of the tree, and tore the moss from it with his nails. The dinner bell called the couple away. Their faces were scarcely visible in the dusk. But he could see enough to realize that on May's there was a look of utter serenity, and a new softness which had smoothed away something of its former angularity. Her lips which once had been too thin and rather colourless, looked now as though they had been swelled with blood. Her lids were heavier than Claude remembered them, and made her eyes seem smaller. Too little sleep had given them an air of languor.

He did not bother to conceal himself, so obvious was it that this young woman no longer knew him, that she had nothing in common with the wild, trapped creature whose pride he had seen humiliated before him one summer's morning. But not yet did he feel the full impact of his pain. He ate as usual, conscious of nothing, until Favereau and Maria, Fourtille and Abel, began to talk about the bride and groom. The things they said were dirty and they went into the most precise details. Fourtille maintained that there weren't any flies on Monsieur Marcel, she was pretty sure of that. . . .

Claude made his escape. He forced himself to look at a star which hung above the roof, at the dark mass of fowls roosting in the pear tree. He could have counted the glittering pebbles on the gravel path, so intently was he concentrating all his mind on external objects so as to postpone the moment when all that was not his appalling agony would collapse about him. The world of appearances was too thin to keep it out. He could feel it coming closer like a burning fire. Though there was not much daylight left, he cut off the dead roses and pruned the bushes. A laugh came from the open windows of the drawing-room, the notes of a piano, a voice. A song, for him no longer, spread about the garden, where now no hungry heart was listening. That passion would for ever be another man's delight. The sound of her voice swept away all the appearances to which Claude had been clinging. In what dark water could he fling himself, and drown? The pond was not deep enough. He had no gun, and, even if he had, could not have used it, for he had strength for nothing but to slip, with closed eyes and out-stretched arms, into the depths. Then he remembered that the river was not far away. A vague scarf of mist out on the plain showed where it ran. Half an hour's walk, and all would be over, but that half hour still lay ahead. He reached the road and started to run. Dogs in the trellized vines began to bark. Oh! to sleep, to sleep! . . .

The wind was getting up, heavy clouds were racing across the sky under the moon, but it was as though she, silent and limpid were travelling, not they. The road was empty. Claude, now short of breath, had to slow down. His crazy thoughts attuned their motion to that of his limbs. He began to think. It was in blind pursuit of sleep and nothingness that he was driving on. But could he be sure that death was sleep or even nothingness? He stopped, and leaned against a chestnut by the roadside. The dampness of the nearby river cooled his face. He breathed in the smell of wet mint and mud, of all the river scents exaggerated in the darkness. He was half way, now, between Lur and the river. Would death bring him the nothingness he longed for? He rubbed his forehead and his hands against the tree's rough bark. The sensation was one which he had always associated with those miserable moments of his childhood when, in flight from the grown-ups, he had leaned his arm against a trunk and cried, finding in it a silent comforter. It is not possible for anyone to escape from life – that was what he feared. We are for ever part of life. If he flung himself into those sluggish waters, what they would carry down to the Atlantic Ocean would not be that part of himself which now was all despair and suffering. The only consequence of his act would be to take despair with him into eternity. No, there was no escape. For death spans life as a bridge spans a river, and once the waters have moved beyond the shadows cast by the piles, they flow on for ever in the light. To escape out of time and space, out of the world of green and blue appearances, of hard earth and solid wood, of stones and grass, is not to escape from life. It is not given to man to decide the moment of his own departure.

Claude had recovered the power of thought. He let his mind go back to what had caused in him this uprush of all the forces of destruction. He saw once more the look he had hoped to see upon her face, of bitterness, of wildness, of frustration, and compared it with what he had actually seen only a short while ago – languor, and heavy, bestial lassitude – for that was all she could have found in the arms of her fat and fleshy husband. Pleasure? *that* pleasure for her, for May? He heard the sound of his own laughter in the darkness. That pleasure, to be sure,

can conjure nothingness, and bring it back again, night after
night, can prolong it with drink and drugs. He remembered
nights of orgy when he was a soldier, the sense of power when
the bottle had been emptied, the sight of a pal scraping away
at a banjo on a corner of the table, of drunken women dancing.
He looked at the lights of Toulenne reflected in the river. Less
than a mile separated him from delights less to be feared than
death. He wanted to run, but, clear-headed now, thought of the
hideous waking in the morning, of the return home, of his
father's laughter and, more than all else, of his mother's indul-
gent kindliness. Suddenly, rain began to fall upon the tree
which sheltered him, but not a drop came through the thick-
set foliage. The night was filled with the murmur of moving
waters: the earth seemed newly waked, and offering to the
rain her most secret fragrances. Claude put his coat over his
head and turned for home. He walked through cool mud.
Sometimes a puddle struck cold to his feet through the rope
soles of his shoes. Long before he reached Lur he saw a light
shining between the trees, the only visible light at that hour.
He knew what room it shone on, and what bed, what couple
not yet ready to give themselves to sleep. A solitude of
drenched fields lay about the lovers. No doubt the falling rain
upon the roof-tiles and the leaves was making a monotonous
sound which, like a vague sigh of love, lay about two beings
now made for ever one in the flesh. No matter how proud a
woman may be, thought Claude, all that she asks of a husband
is that he shall be young, and know how best to give her
pleasure. Even the haughtiest adores the confining bonds of two
male arms, so long as they are not weak. For the happiness of
sleeping on a husband's breast mystics will renounce their love
of solitude, of unshared perfection. He made his way through a
hole in a hedge. A dog barked, then, seeing who it was, yapped
happily. He reached the terrace, and sat there with his legs

dangling over the wall. The rain had soaked his clothes, but he stayed where he was, incapable of movement. He was filled with envy of the quiet trees and their rustling leaves. He wished that some god of the night, filled with pity, would set him in the earth, there to stand unmoving, with deep roots sunk into the soil, and no voice, no gesture, but only the trembling and swaying of high branches in the rainy wind. A blackbird sang, and there was a flutter of wings among the wet leaves, an interrupted trill, the creak of a wagon. A hare, two hares, moved across the meadow below the terrace, making their way in a series of little bounds towards the vines. Some swallows, scarcely out of the nest, were twittering on a branch, while their mother hopped round the open, yellow beaks. From somewhere high up a bell tinkled. Among the vines the cowmen were taking advantage of the hours before the heat of the day set in. Claude washed his hands and face at the trough. His very fatigue made him feel light and empty. The terrible night had, as it were, made him jettison his despair. He wanted to live, to give himself body and soul to the earth, to let mere physical existence stupefy his senses, to attach himself to this patch of soil as completely as any vine-plant or leafy fig-tree. He dropped into a sweet-smelling hayrick, and, after a little preliminary shivering, fell asleep.

"Hey! lazybones, coming to give me a hand with the spraying?"

He got up and followed his father, who strapped a sulphate container to his back. He would have to spend his whole day working his way up and down the vine ridges, stumbling over lumps of earth, in spite of the terrible night he had been through. Gladly he accepted the back-breaking labour, happy to know that when evening came sleep would fall on him before he had had time to cry. The card-house of his love had fallen flat! Sooner or later, no doubt, he would free himself from the satisfied, the sated, May, or rather, it was she who, like a mirage of youth and purity, would melt away. The young girls we have loved die in the arms of the men who possess them. Of that embrace is born a woman whom we no longer know. Iphigenia vanishes in the fire, and nothing is left in her place but a timid, shivering animal.

So thought Claude. Fresh leaves were glittering on the young poplars like the armour of newly-fledged warriors. The distant storm-clouds lifted from the summits of the hills. The wind set a polish on the silky grasslands. One small cloud got between the vineyards and the sun, and the bare hillside was swept with sudden rain. The flooded river looked like liquid mud, and the light of heaven was misted over in the oozy gloom of the waters.

XIII

MADAME GONZALES waited until the daily woman had left the room. Careful as ever, she flung the door open just in order to make sure that no servant's ear was pressed to the keyhole. Only then did she venture to give her daughter a kiss, for the tradespeople had been led to believe that she was no more than a favourite masseuse. The young woman submitted her powerfully built back and loins to the skilful ministrations of the matron, who proceeded to dust talcum powder on this flesh of her flesh. She was full of grievances. She had always known how it would be: Edward was coughing up much less than had been expected. Edith replied that, on the other hand, he had given her more than she could ever have hoped for – an assured position in society. Without him she would have got nowhere.

"That's as may be, my dear; but you've climbed so high now that he can only harm you. There's already talk about his keeping you. That sort of thing holds those with serious intentions at a distance, men like that pepper-and-salt diplomat, Jacques Berbinot – and how charming he is! – who'd marry you like a shot. Edward's meant nothing to you for a long time now, and he doesn't even pretend that he cares two pins about you!"

"That doesn't alter the fact that I'm as necessary to him as the air he breathes! His neurasthenia's getting a terrible hold on him. He's always dangling round me, and if, now and again, I take the risk of going round to see him in the rue de Bellechasse, he just won't let me come away."

"My pet, you ought to make it quite clear to him that he's got, as they say, to take it or leave it – marriage or nothing."

"He'd rather die!"

"Well, then, you'd better become Madame Jacques Berbinot. Things can't go on like this. I hear a good deal in the shop: I encourage my clients to talk. At the moment, you're all the rage, and people are willing to shut their eyes to your somewhat ambiguous situation – but it needs only a real blow up. Oh! I know you've got your head screwed on the right way, but accidents do happen no matter how careful you may be, and then! . . . in the sort of network you live in, only one stitch has got to go, and the rest follow!"

Edith turned over and presented a sagging breast to her mother's hands. She gazed at the ceiling, and thought deeply.

No doubt about it, she had sailed a pretty skilful course. Far-seeing though she was, and careful to avoid all scandal, she was not averse to letting her flat be used as a meeting-place for Orpheus and Eurydice, and even for Socrates and Alcibiades. Fashionable folk, and an occasional artist, played more than one sort of game under her roof. Not that there was any hint of impropriety in what was said. Even a lady like Madame Castagnède could have found no cause for scandal. Perhaps, now and again, those who stayed late were a trifle – but only a trifle – under the influence of port. One evening Edward had noticed that Edith no longer had any need of rouge, so flushed was she as a result of her incursions into that most accessible of all short cuts to Paradise – the Sandeman road. She had owed the beginnings of her good fortune to a clever campaign of log-rolling when her poems appeared. This success had been carried a step further when one of Edward's friends had developed an infatuation for her – a certain Comtesse de La Borde, who, though she was very rich, allowed herself to be kept by a South American. Under her wing Edith had got to know all that section of the smart world which aspired to the "free" life. This miraculous catch had made it unnecessary for her to go on fishing. She called the La Borde circle her "breeding ground of duchesses". . . . The denizens of the fashionable world, who have no very sure sense of values, treated her as though she were a second Madame de Staël. The bewildering complexity of her sayings, the airs of a High Priestess which she affected, were thought to be deeply impressive. Since she kept her telephone at her bedside, all the scandal of the town flowed into the restricted area of her bedroom as unceasingly as though it had been a telephone exchange. She was in a position to compare the varying versions of every new case of adultery or homosexuality. She had perfected an exegesis of gossip and had learned to apply the processes of scientific analysis to scandal. Nor was that all. She had become a prudent, even a discreet, recipient of the most solemn secrets. Since she never tore up any letter, was a past mistress in the accumulation of notes, and a born keeper of files, she was armed to the teeth, and a constant menace. She knew how to make herself feared by those whose hatred she could not overcome.

Surrounded at first by minor poets, who carried about with them their first books of verse as a chick carries one half of its shell, she went on to exhibit in public some of her "dear masters". An author could not visit her without being sure to see on the piano his last published work, or the number of the periodical in which his most recent article had appeared. The book opened of its own accord at the dedication. She knew, none better, how to impose silence when a wit was in labour with an anecdote. If the telling phrase fell flat, she would pick it up, elaborate it, gain for it a victory at second hand. She could make each one of her "exhibits" feel that he was her favourite. An indefatigable listener, she would fall into raptures, clasp the hand of a poet in silent ecstasy with the air of one who could bear no more, and murmur: "The one really great poem of our times!"

Edith did not gratify her mother with words of appreciation, but the old lady's experience had its effect upon her, and she determined to follow her advice. Edward *might* take the easiest way out and dwindle into marriage. It was certainly all or nothing for the poor wretch.

One morning, feeling physically at ease in a loose wrap, Edward lit a cigarette, rang for clean brushes, and started to work on a portrait of Madame de La Borde, from a sketch he had made of her on an occasion when he had been feeling on top of the world and full of self-confidence. But now, every touch he laid upon the canvas made him only too well aware of his technical skill and his whole bag of tricks. He felt that he would never get free from his awful facility, his modish compositions, and those effects which made the philistines gasp, but those who really knew what was what shrug their shoulders in disgust. As he worked, he let his mind play with the most extravagent of possibilities. Perhaps, after all, he *would* succeed in getting out of his dreary rut, *would* stop saying the same thing over and over again, *would* give up copying nature, and even trying to interpret it. The brushes fell from his fingers. Had he, in his best moments, ever really succeeded in escaping from himself? All he had ever asked of art was that it should make him feel a little less dead, should keep him from being swept too rapidly away by the vast tide of obscurity, that it should win him sympathy and admiration. But an artist must be, first and foremost, disinterested. 'What about the others?' he wondered, 'what about the men who crowd round Edith, using art as their pretext, though, with them, it is merely an excuse for playing variations on the theme of physical pleasure. Devotees of passion, they pursue art as a means of giving new turns to the same old sensation.'

Others . . . and here Edward thought of Claude Favereau. Ah! he was different! . . . For him there was a fixed point in the flux of time, an immutable, eternal principle, a tree of salvation standing above the moving waters. 'I'm not surprised,' he thought, 'that the idea of a return to God is so widespread to-day. What makes so many people long for certainty is nothing but the instinct of self-preservation. But when one questions them about faith they tell one that the first essential is grace. My education has made it for ever impossible for me to admit the historical truth of Christianity. I remember, when I was fifteen, attending a course of lectures on Biblical Exegesis, in which each separate verse of the synoptic gospels was submitted to minute examination, undermined, and suspected of being an interpolation. . . . Is the gift of grace arbitrary? They say that one can make oneself worthy of it by prayer. If one turns the handle the right way, all the rest will follow. But the turning of the handle implies an antecedent grace . . . a vicious circle!'

Was he cursed with a temperament which made him incapable of pursuing worldly or political ambitions, small matters which weighted the heart and kept it from rising? For Edward was a balloonist who unloaded his ballast too rashly. He had cut himself adrift from everything which holds a man firmly to the ground. With the violence of a newly-made convert he had attacked his idols and cut his supports from under him. Thus did Polyeucte overturn the false gods and, having broken with the conditions of his pagan past, torn down every bridge which linked him with the "living streams of joy", and found himself left with the one and only God. But Edward, lacking the belief of a Father in Heaven, had lost even the certainty that he would find peace in nothingness and an eternal silence. He felt that he was part of Time, and that the movement of the Universe was carrying him he knew not whither. . . . He could imagine a thousand possible existences, but felt never the faintest hint of a desire to identify himself with any one of them.

He had reached a point at which he could not bear to read a doctrinaire paper. Why should one work oneself into a state about race or country when it needed only a few centuries to change the face of the world? The nationalists of Nineveh and Babylon took his mind from those of Paris. Far from welcoming this attitude of his, he felt as much ashamed of it as he would have done of some physical blemish, some vice. Merely to formulate it made him laugh. . . .

If only he were not shut out from Lur! There he could have sought a refuge with Claude from his broken-down heart. In the whole vast world nothing called to him so insistently as

did the terrace as it must be looking in these Springtime days:
the limes still bare, but the hornbeams in the grove already in
leaf, the sun bringing out the lizards with their throbbing
throats to bask on the old stones, and the cicadas never silenced,
not even by the coming on of night, the single, liquid notes of
birds, the piercing crow of distant cocks, the cowman's voice
urging Caubet and Lauret along the vine rows. It was the time
of the year when the Spring ploughing would be under way,
when the vines must be cut back. Small buds would be showing
on the older plants, and the nights, lit by a red moon, would
hold a threat of frost. The country folk would be moving
among the vines with cauldrons of burning tar to cover the
plants with a heavy smoke to protect them against the cold.
No roses yet, nor fruit. The leaves on the fig-trees, like tiny
hands, would be turning their palms towards the sun. The
river, as a rule invisible, would be in flood, spreading across the
plain like a pool of mercury, the lines of its banks like the edges
of a broken window pane. The tops of the drowned trees would
be lying quietly on its surface, and, in the west, a bank of
yellow cloud be massing in the sky. The grass, where the sunshine touched it, would be gleaming with an intense, an almost
sickly, green. The plain would be soaking up the river like a
sheet of blotting-paper. The dark line of the horizon would
mark the limit of the clouds' wild coursing. From the terrace
one would be able to see the separate onset of three different
storms: one would burst over Les Landes, one threaten
Sauternes, one move straight towards Lur. The far-off squalls,
merging earth and sky, would be marching onwards like an
army, and one would hear the growing sound of falling
rain before so much as a drop had wetted the trees close
by. . . .

Because last night he had suffered from insomnia, Edward
had taken some chloral, and the effects were just beginning to

make themselves felt. He stretched himself out on the sofa, closed his eyes, and fell asleep.

Very quietly Edith came into the studio. She gazed at her sleeping lover, and saw how much older he looked. The harsh daylight showed each line upon his forehead and at the corners of his mouth. His hair was thinning. When she leaned over him she noticed that his breath smelt bad. The youthfulness which she had loved so much was falling apart before her eyes. The mark of rottenness on the fair fruit was barely visible as yet, but how could she fail to notice it, passionate as she was for youth, and for young, unsullied bodies? Now that the bloom was going she knew that nothing of her love remained. No trace of tenderness, she thought, would make her feel regret for doing what she meant to do. Without waking him, she went and leaned upon the balcony. He opened his eyes. Even before he saw her he knew that she was there. Her black silk bag was hanging on the back of one of his chairs. A number of small parcels, a pair of gloves, a handkerchief were lying on an unfinished letter. He got up and stretched. There was a sour taste in his mouth. Edith smiled at him from the French window. Paris had made her seem younger, or, rather, it had "fixed" her youth, giving a sort of eternity to her twenty-eight years. Like so many Parisian women she would benefit from this indeterminate period . . . time would not dim her golden hair: only her neck and breast showed that the science at which Madame Gonzalez excelled was not infallible. When at last she spoke, it was as though she were addressing a child: not feeling quite the thing? not getting on with his work? She looked at the sketch and pulled a face.

"You see, even for the painter solitude is useless."

She sat down beside him, took his hand, and sighed.

"You're my own little man. . . . I'm worried about you. . . . I feel that I must never leave you . . . you know it, too."

He was afraid she was going to suggest that they should live together.

"Remember, Edith, how mis able we were when you lived here with me."

She retorted sharply that she certainly did not want to repeat *that* experiment. Besides, her position now made such a thing impossible. But wasn't there some simpler way of being together without imperilling their independence?

He looked a question. She was choosing her words very carefully. Why shouldn't they try a more successful form of partnership? She would be someone for him to lean on, some-one to save him from himself, to protect him. No reason why they shouldn't have separate rooms, and each respect the other's freedom.

She looked into his eyes. She was not very far from tears, and sat waiting for some sign, however faint, of acquiescence. He decided that he must destroy this hope of hers, once and for all. He forced a laugh, and said in a loud voice: "You're pulling my leg!" – ashamed of breaking with her for good with so vulgar a phrase.

"Why should you think that, Edward? I would get you out of your neurasthenia – I've will enough for two: I would steer your boat for you: your salon would be one of the most frequented in all Paris. *You* won't have the worst of the bargain! Besides, my poor dear, I'm not at all sure that, for you, it isn't quite simply a question of me or death!"

Seized by panic, Edward shouted that death would be preferable:

"I'd far rather die a thousand times!" She got up. Her lower lip was trembling slightly. Edward dared not look at her eyes which suddenly gleamed yellow, at her nose which she was wrinkling like a vicious cat. Behind a false air of nonchalance she was concealing the hatred which for days had been smouldering within her, and now, in a brief moment, burst into flames.

"You're just a spoilt child! Let's say no more about it. I was only thinking of you, and your refusal takes a great weight off my mind, my dear. Only, you'd better not come and see me quite so often: your attentions are doing me a lot of harm. Good-bye."

She held out her hand. He had no illusions. He knew that, during these few months in Paris, the deep-seated ferocity of Edith's nature had been undergoing a careful process of cultivation. The instinct of self-protection, of self-preservation, develops in women who have no one but themselves to look to, a calculated savagery, a subtlety of graded spitefulness, which can progress through all the stages leading from simple backbiting to spiritual murder. Edith's scale of personal values was simplicity itself: she recognized in those about her only allies, benevolent neutrals, suspect neutrals, and enemies.

From now on, when anybody asked Edith for news of Edward, she heaved a deep sigh, and declared that it was impossible for her to answer that question.

"What *can* I say, my dear? He's becoming quite impossible. People of his sort are unendurable unless they contribute something to one's amusement."

"Come off it, Edith!" Madame Tziegel said to her one day with brutal frankness, "You can't get away with that! Come on, out with it: you *did* live with him once, didn't you?"

Whereupon, Edith had broken into a fit of nervous laughter. How could one "live with" a man like Edward Dupont-Gunther? It had never occurred to her, she said, that there could have been any gossip of that kind: it was so absolutely out of the question! – and, with her hand in front of her mouth, she had proceeded to whisper scandal into the other's ear. . . .

But Madame Tziegel would not let the matter drop.

"You must have known what people were saying – didn't you?"

"People will say anything. I didn't undeceive them, out of consideration for him – that's the sort of person I am, darling. No one knows what it cost me. Gossip of that kind did me a good deal of harm, but it helped him a lot – it was a sort of an alibi, if you see what I mean. But I've had about enough of it: I just can't go on: he really has become impossible."

A month later this verdict had taken on the force of law for the whole of her set: no doubt about it, Edward Dupont-Gunther had become impossible. There was no pleasure to be found in his company: he had ceased to be amusing. He could no longer bring himself even to ask anybody round for a drink, and his presence cast a gloom on any party, no matter how high-spirited. He had lost the gift of leaving his mask of tragedy with his coat and hat. It was generally agreed that he had the evil eye. Besides, how could one put up with a man who was for ever talking of killing himself and never doing it?

Edward was like a blind man whose groping hands could no longer find anything solid to touch. Post after post went by without his receiving a single letter. For days together he never opened his lips. Like a condemned criminal who sees his fellow men through bars, he would sit in restaurants, watching other people dining together, talking and laughing. He remembered how, when, as a boy of five, he had sat in form, with the drone of lessons in his ears, and his hands making damp patches on his History of France, he had been filled with envy of the barrow-boys crying their wares in the street. Even the café waiters and restaurant door-keepers had seemed to him to be the happiest of mortals.

He had never believed it possible to live without Edith. He was her prisoner, just as much as a prisoner in a fortress who eats his heart out knowing that there are precipices on every side. He clung to her as a man with a fear of heights will cling to a railing. The hours they spent in idle chatter, the days wasted in a thousand trivial occupations, in meetings and in pointless goings to and fro, were so many ivy tendrils binding him to life. At night he found comfort in her familiar face. He longed for her to be there, like a child who cannot go to sleep unless he knows that he can hear beside him the breathing of the nurse-maid for whom he has no feeling of affection. Cast out by Edith, he dreamed of her drawing-room to which he no longer had the right of entry, conjuring up in imagination the various portraits of her hanging on the walls, signed with the names of painters whom he knew, the sham Coromandel screens, the Russian Ballet divan, the copies of Plato's *Symposium* and Spinoza's *Ethics* lying permanently open on the table. . . . Cigarettes everywhere, port, and all that a man is pleased to find at any hour of the day, so that he is always happy to climb these stairs rather than others. Edward was amazed to find that he could breathe away from the atmosphere of tobacco-smoke and flowers and Guerlain's latest scent, away from her dressing-room and the wardrobes packed with her dresses. He would spend whole days on his sofa, drugging himself with chloral, when night came. He wrote to Firmin Pacaud: "I have a feeling that I have outlived myself". His friend, who was in London on business, did not reply. A letter reached him on Carlton Hotel notepaper, from Biarritz. It was from May, who had done her best to write affectionately. She had begun it at the very bottom of the first page, and he could guess how she must have racked her brains to find enough to fill the sheet. He noticed how her writing had changed and was now modelled on Marcel Castagnède's neat calligraphy.

A man owned her and had destroyed what once she was, to mould her anew in his own image, to shape her to his own likeness.

XIV

ON this June evening the asphalt seemed to be melting, turning to dust, mingling with the smell of horses and petrol. Edward had had a bath and put on for the first time a grey suit with flecks of blue, which fitted closely to his figure. He felt better, and set about blowing the little spark of life within him into a flame. He played in imagination with the possibility of some new adventure, some unexpected meeting, which would put him on terms again with life. On the terrace in front of Fouquet's he changed greetings, and even a hand-shake, with a friend of his who, unfortunately, had a woman in tow. He would have liked to stick with him all evening. All the same, he drank his cocktail in a mood of determined optimism. At the moment, the prospect of spending an evening in the vague hope of a casual encounter, seemed to exhaust his energies. A sick man can live on nothing: a drowning man will snatch at a straw. Round about eight o'clock he began to feel hungry. It was ages since he had had any appetite. He decided to treat himself to a dinner of the kind he liked at the Italian restaurant in the Avenue Matignon. He walked slowly. The feeling that an invisible hand was clutching the back of his neck had become less marked. His enemy was giving him a respite. Walking was no longer an effort. He felt no discomfort in his legs and arms. He was free of the lassitude which sometimes confined him to his sofa for days on end, as rigid as a paralytic. He actually felt young, a young man among other young men, and smiled at a working-girl who had turned her head. Ah! he should have remembered the torture of hope imagined by Villiers: the story of the prisoner who finds the door of his cell open, the corridor empty, no sentry in the yard, who, wild with delight at the prospect of freedom, reaches the last door only to find his tormentor waiting for him with a grin on his face.

All the tables on the pavement were occupied. The head-waiter made a sign to him that there was just one vacant place inside. He ordered one of those *pasta* dishes which he loved because they reminded him of Florence and Naples. As he was filling his glass with iced Asti, he gave a start: he had just caught sight of Edith Gonzales, Madame Tziegel, and Berbinot dining together at a nearby table. He was preparing to smile, and waved a sketchy greeting. He was quite sure that they had seen him, just as he had no doubt at all that it was of him they were whispering with their three heads close together. He had caught that movement of the eyes with which women of the world manage to take in everything without turning round. He stared at them in vain. He began to enjoy himself. Edith was watching her lover's dumbshow in a mirror. She knew him too well not to realize from the expression on his face that he was in the grip of one of his whims, that he was feverishly determined not to let them get away without a smile or a word. He was close enough to his old friends to catch a little of their conversation. Edith was treating them to one of her familiar dissertations on the subject of her gift for being able to tell what people were like from their faces. Berbinot was listening very solemnly. Madame Tziegel was letting her friend "put on her seduction act" – as she called it – but from the way in which she was resting her chin on her hand, and her elbow on the table, he could see that she was making no bones about showing how bored she was. By this time, Edith had changed the subject, and was busy extolling in a loud voice the work of a young novelist of her acquaintance.

Madame Tziegel dropped a remark: "There's nobody like Dostoevsky. . . ."

Edward could not hear what Berbinot said, but it must have been something to the effect that he had never read anything the Russian novelist had written, because Madame Tziegel, turning towards him, said, so loudly that the diners at the neighbouring tables could not help hearing her:

"Never read him? – but that's impossible, my dear man! It's as though you told me that you had never taken a bath!"

Edith must have brought out one of her ready-made remarks about Dostoevsky, for Madame Tziegel at once broke in again:

"My dear girl, you don't begin to understand him! Dostoevsky is like life, simple and complex at the same time . . . but I feel too lazy to explain it all to you. . . ."

She relapsed into her former apathy, an started crumbling her bread like a pretty trollop being entertained at a restaurant by two of her more "serious-minded" clients, who bore her to tears.

Edward by this time was losing all patience, and, though he had reached the fruit stage while the others had scarcely begun their dinner, he was determined not to get up until they had left, because they would have to push past his table on their way out. He therefore ordered some coffee and a glass of Armagnac in order to gain time. His torment was made worse by the thought that Edith must know perfectly well what he was going through and be enjoying it and, perhaps, imparting her enjoyment to her friends. She was glutting her hatred, revelling in her vengeance for all she had suffered at Lur from the Dupont-Gunther family, for the humiliations that had been forced upon her. She was now getting her own back, taking her pound of flesh from this wretched, tortured wreck of a man. She had guessed what Edward was at and was deliberately prolonging his agony. She felt sorry when Madame Tziegel gave the signal to move: but they had planned to go and look at the Bois by moonlight, and afterwards to sup at the Pré-Catelan. When they had collected their cloaks they passed close by Edward. Madame Tziegel gave him a slight nod: Edith averted her face.

Edward, in his turn, reached the door. The night was heavy with a threat of storm. He walked like a man suffering from the effects of gas. The orchestra of the Ambassadeurs had drawn a large crowd. Brilliantly lit cars were moving up the Avenue towards the Théatre des Champs-Elysées where there was a Russian Ballet first night. Like a visitor from another world, like a wandering ghost in the land of the living, he looked through the windows at the gorgeously dressed women. He was wrapped in a sort of peace. He felt that he no longer had any part even in his own misery. The idea came to him to go and knock at the door of a friend beyond the Butte who was slowly dying of opium. But he did not feel strong enough to walk that far. People were seated round the *cafés-concerts* listening to the blaring music, the applause, the laughter, and imagining what was happening on the stage they could not see. How long he hung about the groups of small shopkeepers taking the air, he never knew. At last, however, he got up from his chair, walked back to the Concorde, mingled with the crowds on the boulevards, looked in at the Olympia, and sat down at a table. But the women gave him no peace, so he went out again. Sheer weariness compelled him to call a halt at the Café Riche. The place was full of gypsy musicians, idle waiters, shining tables, but, otherwise, not a soul. In the old days he had found a curious pleasure in haunting the solitude which broods over deserted places designed for pleasure. *Maîtres-d'hotel* and waiters settled on him like a swarm of flies. Between each dance a woman dressed in tawdry spangles, sat down beside him and went through her whole dismal repertory of seduction. By this time he was slightly drunk, and felt like crying on her thin shoulder. He called for his bill, walked down the rue Royale, and went into Maxim's. He found himself next to a lot of fat men, wholesale butchers by the look of them, who were obviously out on a spree. There was a time when he could not have stood their company for five minutes: large paunches bulging over thin legs, purple lips, low collars and made-up ties, with dangling trinkets on their watch-chains, making filthy talk with women who quite obviously despised these Saturday-night clients. But now he was the last to leave, and when the rising sun brought the street-cleaners creeping along the walls like lice, and gleamed on wagons loaded with carrots, some instinct drove him to sit down on a bench opposite the Madeleine. He remembered a day when he was twenty, walking home with a friend now dead. They had dropped down, worn out, on a bench, and the boy had put his head on Edward's shoulder and gone to sleep. He remembered how he had watched over his slumber, while the Madeleine grew slowly brighter, standing there at a meeting point of such tremendous solitudes, that it was as though they were sitting in some city found again after a thousand years under a crust of cold lava. Ah! moments of happiness so fragile that the heart watches them go by, though the eyes do not so much as notice them.

A few taxis passed, then an early bus. The young man went into a post-office and wrote a letter to his servant saying that he would not be back for several days. The smell of green growing things and wet branches reached him from the Champs-Elysées, just such a smell as must be rising now from the pleached alley at Lur to meet the rising sun: carnations would be hem-stitching the garden beds with a white fragrance.

Ah! why not throw off his false shame? – why not jump into the Bordeaux train, and return to the last refuge open to him, Claude's heart? – why not go to earth among the vines like a wounded hare when it has thrown the hounds off the scent? He was already running in the direction of the Quai d'Orsay station. He stopped to dip his hands in the cold water of one of the fountains on the square. In imagination he could see his father, that face which was more bestial than those of the fat men whom he had watched in the night hours, laughing, sweating, and drinking with women of the streets. Perhaps he would kick him out, or take pleasure in humiliating him. Edward turned round and walked away from the station. All the same, he must take some sort of a train, must get away, must escape. . . . But where to? Then, as though to prove to himself that he would not yield to the temptation of Lur and of Claude, he hailed a taxi and had himself driven to the Gare de l'Est. He saw a list of places over the window of the booking-office – Epernay, Chalons, Nancy. . . . He asked at random for a first-class to Chalons. In his compartment were two officers, a general and a captain, surrounded by copies of *Le Cri de Paris* and *Le Rire*. They stared hard at the well dressed young man, with unwashed, unshaved face, and a mad look in his eyes, who fell into a heavy sleep almost as soon as he had sat down.

At about the same time, in Bordeaux, May was entering up her private diary:

"Just back from the honeymoon. This unfamiliar apartment seems stranger to me than our hotel room at the Carlton. Reading through this diary I am struck with amazement. I can scarcely recognize my former self. Did I really feel such transports only a few months ago? It isn't that I don't still have qualms of conscience, but they are of a kind I could not put into words even in the pages of this secret book. Oh God! one

cannot yield to the promptings of the flesh with impunity! . . .
Between shame and the sanctified embraces of the marriage
bed how small the difference is! According to Father's instructions I ought to look upon the body with pure eyes. He thinks
that a lurking trace of heresy gets between me and Marcel
who is so regular in his religious observances, doesn't worry
about making sure of the precise limits within which the Church
permits married people to indulge their desires. I have told him
about my uneasy conscience, and of my conviction that God
is more exigent than the theologians. There are forms of
interior humiliation which are *not* illusory. I have a feeling that
I have fallen from grace; I am filled with a sense of disgust with
myself. . . . It wouldn't be so bad if I took no pleasure in that
side of marriage – but I do! and the fact that my pleasure is
legitimate does not console me for its baseness. Father has
imposed on me, as a penitence, the task of meditating St.
John's saying . . . 'if our heart condemn us, God is greater
than our heart.'

"Father would dearly like me to attach more importance to
scruples of a different kind. He knows, from what I have told
him, about Edward and Claude. He is concerned for both those
men, whom he has never seen, because to one of them I am
attached by the bonds of nature, to the other by the circum-
stance of grace. He asks me what I have made of my brother.
It is no use my saying that it is more important for him to
know what it was that my brother was within an ace of
destroying in me. All that is evil in me comes from him, and I
know that the weed which, though I tear it out, grows up
again and flourishes in my heart, was planted there by his
sickly hands. That is why I have no feeling of remorse. Still, in
obedience to my director, I forced myself to write to Edward
from Biarritz. What an effort those three wretched pages cost
me! Another than I, that Edith whom I do try not to hate,

who has taken him from me for ever, will no doubt help him
not to die. It was *he* who abandoned *me*. No, I am not responsible for the state of *his* heart. As to Claude, who managed to
remain so completely hidden during my stay at Lur that I did
not even think of him, I know that he is in the hands of the
Almighty. About his salvation I am not uneasy, for I know
that he is one of the elect, a chosen vessel, and that in him the
Master is well pleased. Was it not through him that I came to
salvation? Yes, for though what was young in both of us was
carnally moved, at a quite different level he opened to me the
door of the Garden, and entered before me into the Kingdom."

When he reached Chalons, Edward failed to find a cab. He
was directed to the *Hôtel de la Haute-Mère-Dieu*, in the middle
of the town, some half-hour's walk from the station. He went
along a dismal suburban street under a fierce noon sun. He
dragged his weary feet through evil-smelling dust, and at last,
yielding to the allurement of a canal in which two thick clumps
of chestnuts were reflected, turned towards it and found himself
in a place which had something of the look of an old-fashioned
garden. Though by this time he was quite lost, it did not occur
to him to ask his way, but wandered on. He noticed one of the
old town gates, and a house in which the sweetness of an older
France still lived on, though barracks and parade grounds had
eaten into the body of the town like an eczema. He crossed the
rue de Marne along which a crowd, mainly consisting of
soldiers, flowed on between shops which had done their best
to acquire a "Paris look". He stopped in front of their windows.
In one he saw a display of sporting guns and revolvers. He
could not tear himself away from it, but stood for a while with
his face pressed to the glass. He put his hand on the door-knob,
then changed his mind and instead went into a nearby barber's.
He waited to be shaved in a company of staring officers. A

captain slipped into the chair and stole his turn, but he did not protest. A flick of the brush on suit and shoes made him look once more like a presentably dressed young man. Reassured by his improved appearance, he plucked up courage, and went into the gunsmith's where he bought a pocket pistol, the action of which the salesman displayed for his benefit. Then he resumed his aimless wandering until, in a dark street, his eye was caught by a sign bearing the words *Hôtel de la Cloche*. He asked for a room, and a greasy waiter showed him into one on the first floor. The curtains and carpet would, at any other time, have made him shudder. It opened on to an outside wooden gallery. An appalling stench came from the lavatories on the various floors. This inner courtyard never saw the sun, and the prevailing smell was of damp chill. The paper on the walls of his room was torn and stained. He sat down and, taking a piece of ruled paper wrote: "I am at the Hôtel de la Cloche, Chalons-sur-Marne. If, in five days from now, that is to say, Sunday midnight, you have not come, I shall clear out." He made a copy of this message on another piece of paper, sealed both envelopes, addressed one to Edith Gonzales, the other to Claude Favereau, and walked round to a tobacconist's shop, where he posted them.

XV

THE month of June, when the drowsy afternoons in the pleached alley were filled with the mingled scent of lime blossom and syringa, restored Claude Favereau to life. Lulled by the drone of the harvester, half fuddled by the smell of the hay, exhausted by the work he had done at loading the wagons (so full that their huge burden, silhouetted against the washed-out blue of the sky, almost completely concealed the oxen, so that nothing of them could be seen but two long straining backs prolonged by four tapering horns), he walked, bare-footed in his rope-soled shoes, in front of the team, with all the dignity of David, the shepherd-boy. The Bengal roses, as though remembering that it was the season of the Corpus Christi, seemed eager to spread their tousled heads in the dust. He filled his lungs with air, and knew that no grief could stand against the intoxicating feeling of being twenty years old and bound to this blessed patch of earth. The parish priest of Viridis had given back to him his peace of mind. He was waiting, quite calmly, for a sign. Besides, at this time of the year the soil must be forced into obedience. The days were too short for all there was to do. No sooner were the vine plants pruned than their roots had to be covered, and scarcely had they been sprayed with sulphate, than it was time to powder with sulphur-dust the flowers which smelt sweeter than mignonette. It was the season of young peas. The cherries had been left to the tender mercy of the birds. There were not enough hands available to empty the overflowing baskets under the blazing blue. While the hayricks filled the shadows with their fragrance, a storm-cloud would push its face of gloom upwards in the south above the purple distance of Les Landes. Already there would be a quivering in the leaves. That the hay might be saved, the meal would be left half eaten, and when, at last the final load was safely under cover, Claude would drop like a felled ox on to his bed and, with the window wide, sleep through the crashing of the thunder and the susurration of the liberating rain.

It was this wholly animal life which saved him. The earth, mastered and moulded by his hands, the earth of which he seemed to be a part, enabled him to tear himself loose from

the obsession of his thought. The former postulant, saved from
temptation by sheer physical fatigue, thanked God each night
for this release in a mingled sigh of weariness and faith which
was all the prayer of which he was capable. On the Thursday
of the Feast of Corpus Christi he carried the canopy out on to
the road which was like a river of fire. In front of all the
houses sheets, looking whiter than the highway, were starred
with camelias less white than the radiance of the Host at the
centre of all this incandescent whiteness. On the wayside altars
stood fine vases from the drawing-rooms of country houses:
brass kitchen candlesticks had emerged from the darkness of
ancient interiors, and their pale flames seemed fixed, as though
made motionless by the Real Presence. Claude, on his way
back, rejoiced because the weight of the canopy exhausted him.
He saw, as he approached them, country people falling to their
knees in the dust.

When he got back to Lur about five o'clock, his mother
gave him a letter. He recognized Edward's handwriting on the
envelope. He did not open it at once, but put it in his pocket,
and went to sit upon the terrace, telling himself that this thin
missive might well contain something that would destroy the
inner peace to which he had so hardly won. There were
moments when he feared that he might come to hate those
whom once he had so dearly loved. One Sunday May had come
to Lur with her husband, and, as he touched his hat, Claude had
felt the old wound ache again. Still, he had come triumphantly
through the ordeal, convinced now that he could go on living
in spite of all his bitter memories. He had been less fearful of
his former love, of May who, married, had become a different
person, than he was of the spirit of evil which was, he felt sure,
contained in this letter. An ugly image had protected him
from the woman he had seen leaning on her husband's arm,
and walking slowly, her face both thinner and fuller than it

had been once, and in her eyes, a dreamlike, sleepy, animal expression. What now remained of the wild young innocent who once had disturbed his heart and thrilled his flesh? Nervously, as though only what was to be dreaded could reach him through the medium of this letter, he tore open the envelope and read: "I am at the Hôtel de la Cloche, Chalons-sur-Marne. If, in five days from now, that is to say, Sunday midnight, you have not come, I shall clear out."

He crumpled the letter and put it back into his pocket. This festal day had filled the countryside with emptiness and silence. He forced himself not to understand the meaning of that "I shall clear out". But the contraction of his throat, and the beating of his heart told him only too well that he had grasped its significance. By what right was that young man involving him in his madness? Already, because of him and of his sister, he had endured long hours of agony, had almost drowned, and now, when he had barely recovered his tranquility, these words from Edward had hurled him back into the abyss. . . . Of one thing he felt certain: he would not go, would not even write. Of what concern to him was this bourgeois, what help could this fine gentleman hope to get from a country lout? . . . In any case, how could he get to Chalons?

"*He'll* never kill himself."

Claude spoke the words aloud, as though the better to convince himself. But even while they were upon his lips, he saw within his mind the face of his young master – the wild eyes, the air of detachment, the remote gleam that seemed to come from a different planet. How could he doubt that the dominant trait in the man's character was dazed bewilderment? – a willing surrender to some deadly seduction more powerful to deceive him than a mirage? Suddenly, he felt overcome by panic. Stronger than any reasoning, the certainty came to him that the two of them were bound indissolubly together, that he was part and parcel of Edward's destiny. One evening, in a moment of atrocious mockery, Edward had expressed the wish that Claude should be his scapegoat. Can we ever be sure how far a thoughtless word may echo?

Why had the mere reading of this letter brought such trouble to his spirit? He no longer had the slightest affection for the young man who once had attracted him as the cool verge of a delicious wood might have done. But scarcely had he set his foot within it than bog, stagnant water, and gloomy silence had sent him scuttling back. This desperate summons roused no soft feelings in him, but only a sense of fearful urgency. Practical-minded and well-balanced, he saw at once the difficulties of an enterprise to which his mystical predisposition seemed likely to commit him. Where could he find the money? Would his father let him go? Was there the slightest chance that he would understand the necessity of such a mission?

Seated on the terrace with his legs dangling, he tried to get some order into his thoughts, forced himself to consider methodically the ways and means at his disposal. All things considered, the best thing he could do, he decided, was to put himself in the hands of the Almighty Will, and let himself be carried like a straw in a great wind. Therefore, he fixed his thoughts on God and, true to the habit he had acquired at the seminary, made a deep silence in himself. With a passionate movement of his whole being he strove to establish contact with that Strength and that Love, in which, as elements external to this world, he had so deep a faith. The silence in his heart was, as it were, a prolongation of that other silence lying upon a countryside emptied of life by Festival. There was something astonishing in the fact that there could be so strong a spiritual impulse within a youth who was so healthy, so sensual, so capable of ardour in his daily avocations. It was this very strangeness that had once attracted Edward, the man who was feeling now that nothing in this world could hold him back from the edge of a great emptiness.

Claude went into the kitchen where his father, dressed in his Sunday best, and with his spectacles on his nose, was reading the agricultural column in *Le Nouvelliste*:

"Says here that you should put sulphur on vines when they're in flower. I done it *afore* that: got it all finished and over."

He had complete confidence in himself, and the most utter contempt for "them bookish chaps". He demanded that he should be listened to as an oracle, and for thirty years his wife had unquestioningly accepted the statements made in so profound a tone by the "old man" – there had never *been* such a thing as phylloxera which was just something *they* had invented. His head was chock full of similar certainties. He was convinced that there was no more honest a bailiff anywhere than he was. He had a keen nose for adultery, incest, and all the crimes in the calendar – but they always took place in someone else's family circle, never in his own. Not that he was malicious, but simply that he wanted to enhance his own importance, and loved to think of himself as a man of exceptional honesty and moral integrity. At sight of that narrow, stubborn forehead, that full, swarthy face, Claude was filled with dismay. Favereau greeted him with a smile – the image of benevolence, a man preserved in the liquor of his own self-confidence, who saw human beings and the great Universe itself in his own image, and judged, in the last analysis, all things in Heaven and on earth with the complacency bred of an inner emptiness. Obviously he could not come within a thousand miles of grasping the urgent need of responding to Edward's cry for help. Still, Edward was his master's son, and Favereau was not in the habit of arguing when it was a matter of carrying out orders. It was in that light, therefore, that Claude decided to present the matter. In as detached a manner as possible he told his father that Mister Edward had something important to say to him, and had instructed him to go to Paris as soon as possible. He had, however, mumbled his words and spoken too quickly. A frown creased the paternal brow.

"I don't like you having secrets with the boss's boy. You must know they've had a fine old row. You go on now and write Mister Edward that he'd better tell you what it is he wants in a letter: then we can both see what's in the wind."

Having judged the situation in the light of his wisdom, Favereau re-adjusted his spectacles and resumed his reading of the paper. Claude realized clearly enough that the subject was closed, and that no appeal could lie against his father's decision. All the same, he made another attempt. Mister Edward, he said, had made a great point about *telling* him in person what it was he wanted. He attached great importance to this interview.

"I'm only asking you to advance me the money for the journey, father. Mister Edward will pay me back, no doubt about that."

"So my fine gentleman wants me to pay for's return ticket, eh? *I* know what you're after. You wants to have a fling in Paris, just when there's more work'n we can get through! There's them vines to be trained proper, and sprayed, and the hay to be got in."

With a wicked glint in his eye and the suppressed chuckle of an old chap "as can't be put upon", he added:

"You're a good lad, and this is the first time you've tried to get money out o' me. You've not got the way of it. Come on, out with it now! there's a bit of skirt mixed up in all this, I'll be bound. No need to be afraid to tell me – it's natural enough for a young fellow. You earns enough to have your bit of fun here. But, oh no! you wants a trip to Paris!"

He laughed, well satisfied that his son should want to have a fling, and proud of his own perspicacity.

"It's not that, father: you're quite wrong. I don't need money, and I don't know why you should think there's a woman mixed up in this. It's all quite simple, really. Mister Edward needs me. After all, I'm not a child, and it wouldn't hurt you to advance me a few francs. . . ."

"I've heard all as I wants to hear!" Favereau was now purple in the face:

"Get out o' here! – I don't want another word from you. What d'you take me for, a . . .?"

Accustomed though he was to the coarsest of barrack-room obscenities, he could not stand hearing them from his father. But he knew it was useless to go on. They lived in two different worlds, and the words they spoke to each other were lost in the intervening space. He left the room. But his mind was made up: somehow or other he would get to Edward. How was he to find the money? Almost the whole of his wages went to Favereau for board and lodging. He was obsessed by the need to start on his journey. He felt quite sure now that this cry for help had been uttered by a man in desperate straits. He imagined Edward sitting at a table with a revolver before him, and a clock in that unknown town sounding the first stroke of midnight. He thought of the soul for which he knew himself to be, in some strange way, responsible, for which he had stood surety, which he alone could hold back from the vast darkness of damnation. To this agony of his was added a newly awakened feeling of tenderness. He remembered the trembling eagerness with which, once, he had waited for his young master to come. What a proof of extraordinary affection that letter was, and how lost and abandoned must he be who had written it be feeling! – unless, of course, it was all a hateful joke, a way of finding out just how far his power over a young country lad extended. But Claude, as he strode through the vineyard towards the sunset, shook his head. He had never really believed in Edward's ferocity. Trained in a school of casuistry, he had, from the first, seen through the wiles of that unhappy temperament, and felt the unplumbed desolation they concealed. 'How utterly lost he must have been feeling' – he thought – 'to see in me his only help in all the world! In what a solitude he must be living! But how am I to find the money?' Suddenly the thought came to him of the abbé Paulet, the parish priest of Viridis. Not that he, probably, was any less poor than himself: still it was a question of no more than a loan for a few days.

Under the lime-trees in the square, inmates of the local orphanage were dismantling the temporary altar, a group of little girls gathering in their pinafores scraps of golden blossom and dead roses. He went straight into the presbytry without knocking. The housekeeper who was washing asparagus told him that the priest was at the school, but would almost certainly be back soon. Because of the procession he had kept his boys and girls rather longer than usual.

Claude went up to the first floor. The priest's room looked out on to the garden which lay on the side of the house away from the square. From the window he could see a pergola on which the roses were already wilting. The first lilies were opening above a mass of more ordinary flowers. At the far end of the box-bordered path stood a small arbour of green leaves. Within it stood a figure of Notre-Dame-de-Lourdes discoloured by damp. He sat down at the writing-table. Absent-mindedly he turned the pages of the *Aquitaine*, trying to concentrate his mind upon a recent homily delivered by the Archbishop. A small iron camp-bedstead stood in one corner of the room. A black screen with a pattern of golden storks in flight only half hid a bottle-encumbered washstand. The glass-fronted bookcase held a number of volumes so neatly arranged that it was clear their owner never touched them. On the table was a breviary stuffed full of First Communion pictures, and a shaving brush with the soap still on it. Behind the glass-domed clock were a number of school photographs, groups of young boys in football clothes, with the abbé in the middle holding a large ball. Claude brooded over this life which might so well have been his own. He felt touched by what he saw, and scared at the thought that he, too, might have become a saint had not the call of flesh and blood been strong in him. . . . Then, once more, his mind went back to Edward. What a gulf lay between that unhappy soul and the spirit of the man for whose return he was waiting! What unknown power was it which, over such great distances, could bring two hearts together? – an illusory distance, however, because both spiritually and materially the priest, beyond a doubt, would help him to save that lost sheep.

But could the abbé Paulet lay hands on the necessary sum? Claude heard a voice in the hall below.

"I never seem to see you now, Claude."

The priest put his two hands on the young man's shoulders. Even when his lips had ceased to smile, the smile lived on in the warmth of the frank and guileless eyes. They alone gave beauty to the rather ordinary face with its undistinguished features and stubbly chin. The thick hair, growing low on the forehead, was showing signs of receding. At once the abbé could see that Claude was deeply troubled, but he let him take his time, and filled the gap by talking of the Corpus Christi procession. What a lovely day! All his boys and girls had communicated: all the little imps had gathered about the Blessed Sacrament.

"But that wasn't all, Claude. The best thing of all happened only just now. When I had left them, I went into the organ-loft to put out the music, and whom should I see in the nave kneeling in front of the Blessed Sacrament, but Raymond

Paillac and Bordes. They didn't know I was there, so it can't have been merely to please me."

"You're doing a wonderful work, abbé." The priest, fearing lest these words should minister to his pride, protested that not to him, but to the Father was glory due.

"And what about you, Claude: it is so long since we met."

Claude considered how he should put his request and, after a moment or two, said, very quickly, like a child in the confessional who hurriedly blurts out the sin he finds it difficult to talk about:

"Abbé, I am desperately in need of fifty francs."

"Fifty francs? why, what's the matter?"

"It's difficult to explain. . . . I doubt whether I could make anybody understand."

"That remains to be seen," replied the priest, very simply. "Tell me what it's all about. No need to rely upon my poor understanding: there's a great light here to help us. Speak without fear, my son. There is someone with us who, from all eternity, has known what is the help you have come here to find."

In a second Claude passed from a mood of uneasiness to one of complete confidence. He had often thought to himself that there must have been many a labouring man who, when he came to die could truthfully say that the only person who had ever been seriously interested in him was this hard-working mission priest, who had taught him to play football when he was twelve years old, and, after the game, had prevailed upon to make confession. And so it was that he found himself talking freely and without any sense of embarrassment. He had already spoken to the abbé about Edward, and this made explanation all the easier. The good father made no attempt to interrupt him, but when Claude gave him the letter from Chalons, he took it, and kept it in his hand far longer than would have been necessary for mere reading. While he was studying it, Claude went on:

"There is something in me, whether good or bad I do not know, which urges me to respond to this appeal. If you lend me the money, I shall still have to defy my father. But I don't dare to think what would happen at Chalons if I did nothing. You do think, don't you, that I ought to go?"

The abbé's only reply was to get up and open a drawer. From it he took a box which had once contained some sort of medicine. In this there was some small change and two fifty franc notes, one of which he held out to Claude.

"I'll pay it back by instalments out of my wages."

A child's head appeared in the opening of the door:

"They're asking for you downstairs, Father, it's for Seconde Hugon: they think she's going to die."

Although the sun had set, Claude could still feel the warmth of the road through his rope soles. Should he take the evening train without saying a word to his father? The wisest course, no doubt, would be not to run the risk of another argument, all the more so because there was no time to lose. Edward had fixed on Sunday midnight as the moment beyond which he would not wait. Claude reckoned that, making full allowance for possible delays, he ought to leave Toulenne by the ten o'clock train that night, so as to catch tomorrow's express from Paris. In that way he would reach Chalons, at latest, on Saturday morning. But the abbé Paulet's approval had given him such a sense of confidence, that he decided it would be unworthy of him to hide his intentions from his father. No, there must be no lying, no deceit before he set out upon his mission. . . .

Favereau was seated on the bench in front of the door with Maria, whose two hands crossed idly on her apron, showed that this was a Feast Day on which no work was done. She called out to her son that they had finished supper, but that she had put some soup and cold meat aside for him.

"Whoever heard of a young fellow going off on the loose and forgetting to have something to eat and drink first! Go on, lad, and tuck in."

"I'm not hungry, father."

Favereau thought that Claude was sulking. In his old sergeant-major's voice he announced that that sort of thing didn't go down with him. Claude looked at the narrow forehead and the pendent dewlaps. Very quietly he said:

"The thought of catching the train has taken away my appetite. It's no good you getting angry. I'm not a child: I know what I've got to do. I *must* start this evening!"

"Oh, so you must start this evening!" Favereau was choking with fury, but he managed to keep enough of his bantering tone to say:

"Travelling free, I suppose?"

"Don't worry: I've got all I need."

"So you've found some money, eh? Well, you can take it from me that you're not stirring out of this house. Who gives the orders here? When I've made up my mind about a thing, it's not likely I'd change it for a snivelling brat like you! What I've said, I've said!"

He was on his feet now, and roughly pushed Maria away when she tried to intervene.

Claude felt his own temper rising. He elbowed his way past his father, and started to go upstairs. Favereau was hot on his heels like an old dog.

"You're not going, I tell you! or, if you do, you'll not come back here!"

Claude backed into his room. His father had relapsed into silence. A sudden idea had calmed him. The young man sat down on his bed, though not for a moment did he take his eyes from his father's face. Suddenly, the old man took the key from the lock, went out, and slammed the door behind him. The key turned before Claude could do anything. He was a prisoner.

"Just you go, my lad, just you go! you can jump out of the window for all I care! but you won't get no train this evening!"

He stumped downstairs, Claude shook the door. The old man came on his wife listening, and shaking all over. He burst out laughing, but there was an ugly look on his face.

"Bring me a litre!"

"But, Favereau, the boy. . . ."

"Didn't you hear what I said? Bring me a litre!"

She obeyed without another word. Her husband spent the evening drinking. Not a sound came from the room in which Claude was confined.

XVI

WHEN Edith woke up her first thought was that Madame Tziegel had not asked her to the dinner-party she was giving for Gennaro. Ever since the great Dalmatian poet had arrived in Paris, the fashionable world had been competing for the honour of supplying him with free nourishment. He must be dining every night in a different house. Edith had carefully checked off the tables at which it seemed likely that he might still fill the role of distinguished guest. She had begun to notice that she was never asked out nowadays except by telephone at the last moment, to fill a gap, or to small impromptu gatherings. But it wasn't too much to expect that Madame Tziegel, at least, would give her due notice. The fact that she had not once met Gennaro at dinner was making her position as a Muse difficult, and even slightly ridiculous. An invitation at the eleventh hour, however, was still possible. Her friend, she knew, was enough of a bitch to let her chew the cud of her grievance for as long as possible. She decided not to go near the telephone just in case Madame Tziegel should ring, and find the line engaged. She got up, slipped on a dressing-gown, sat down in front of her looking-glass, and proceeded, without any illusions, to take stock of herself. . . . She felt worn out. All this bogus luxury was getting her down. It was bad enough if one had a maid to dress one, a car to take one calling, and always ready when one went out in the evening, gliding and shimmering through the empty streets, no matter what the hour, just when it was needed. In the case of rich women, everything they could dream of was there to help them, from the bathroom, where the water was always hot, to the bed where they could sleep off the fumes of champagne. But that sort of existence was a heavy load for a young woman to carry who had just *got* to cultivate the friendship of some wretched female she cared nothing about, and to arrange for her to be invited everywhere, for no better reason than that they both lived in the same part of the town, and the "friend" had a car, which was a great help when it came to going home. Edith looked at her stale morning body. A sharp attack of rheumatism had confined old mother Gonzales to her bed. Edith had lost her only slave.

"Your hot water, Mademoiselle, and the post." She could hear outside the door the sound of a jug being put down on the floor. She hurriedly went through her letters, to see whether there was an envelope bearing Madame Tziegel's crest. She was surprised to see Edward's handwriting. At this particular moment, when she was feeling abandoned by all her friends, it gave her a little pang of pleasure. At first, not grasping what it meant, she read through the same formula which was destined, at the other end of France, to bring such perturbation to Claude. But little by little the full sense of that cry for help got through to her mind, and since, for the last hour the young woman had been pitying herself, she found it easy to feel pity for her lover. Had she been in a happy mood, she would merely have shrugged and smiled. As it was, however, conscious that she was beaten and at the end of her tether, she could afford a little sympathy for somebody else in the same boat. Not that she really believed that he would be as good as his word: still, he must be going through an awful time. Humiliated as she was, it was something to know that she filled so large a place in the life of any man. Since she was, more than anything else, practical, and knew how precarious her existence was, she immediately decided to make it up with him, and began at once to work out a design for living somewhere far from this social whirl. Nothing could well be worse. She consulted a time-table, and arranged to start that evening, or the following morning. Instead of sitting at dinner with a lot of snobs, she would fly to her despairing lover. The contrast gave her a sense of nobility: she felt superior to the folk among whom she lived, and became distinctly sentimental. She was proud to think how well she was behaving, flattered, and, at the same time, slightly ashamed that her conduct at the Italian restaurant should have had this devastating effect upon the melancholy Edward. Glad to have been diverted from her own gloomy broodings, she gave her mind entirely to this new plan for the future, bringing to it all her instinctive gift for practical affairs, and her fondness for a good fight.

She lay down on her bed which, in the daytime served the purposes of a sofa. The ringing of the telephone brought her to her feet. So violently was her hand shaking that she could

barely lift the receiver. Oh! joy of joys! it really was Madame
Tziegel's voice this time.

"I don't know what can have come over me, darling: I
don't believe I ever told you that I was counting on you for
lunch. . . . Gennaro's coming . . . no, not to-day . . . the
day after to-morrow . . . yes, Friday."

"I wasn't expecting anything of the sort, dear friend. Anyhow, Madame Obligado is inviting me one day this week to
meet the great man."

Madame Tziegel knew this was not true, and was on the
point of replying that, in that case, since she could accommo-
date only a limited number of guests, she would cancel the
invitation, because Edith would be seeing the poet elsewhere.
She hesitated, however. Cruel she might be, but she did not like
the idea that her cruelty might bring down jeremiads on her
head.

"Then you will meet him twice, my dear."

Edith reflected that she could start for Chalons on Friday
evening, and thus arrive twenty-four hours before the ultimatum expired. That settled, she gave her whole mind to
thinking what she should wear.

The great man helped himself twice to every dish, blossomed
forth, snuffed up the proffered incense, and tucked away enough
homage to keep him going through the eight months he would
have to spend in Dalmatia. He rolled his r's, enjoyed listening to
his own voice, and was delighted to think that he could make
people laugh much more freely in Paris than he could at home,
blissfully ignoring the fact that it was his gesturing and his
accent, rather than his anecdotes that were responsible. Edith,
already distinctly under the influence of champagne cup, let
her head, with its burning cheeks, droop forward, and with a
Pre-Raphaelitish movement, carried a lily to her nose. She

was there: she had "arrived"! A young painter was explaining
Cubism to Gennaro.

"I first concentrate on the tones, you see: then I enclose them
in a series of shapes – a pipe, a tube, it doesn't much matter
what, and so build up my composition, giving to it a pattern
that shall express my essential ego. There are certain wallpapers
to be found in country lavatories which are of a quite adorable
blue. It's not – you do agree, don't you? – worth taking a lot
of trouble to make reproductions of the Crown Jewels. For
me the cardboard binding of an old account-book, or a pipe,
means more than a Holy Family."

No, the poet did *not* understand. True, he was not listening
very attentively. He found the lady next to him more than a
little disturbing. Fruit, in his case, could never be too ripe.
Not, however, having much social experience, he could not
disguise the state of his feelings. The white hair of the enchant-
ing Bolivian set off her limpid, childlike eyes to perfection.

Through the delicious shimmer of her various and somewhat
confused sensations, the prospect of the journey on which she
was to embark in two days time, flashed into Edith's consciousness. It had lost any charm it might once have had. After all, she
had accepted the idea only as a sort of second-best at a moment
when she had been feeling more than usually out of things.
Sitting at this table, surrounded by luxury, she shuddered at
the prospect of having to start on a journey at six a.m., of
arriving in a strange town, and, worst of all, of having to go
through a "scene". Still, go she must, and go she would. But why
spoil present pleasure by dwelling on so distressing a future?

The Bolivian fair one was planning a luncheon party at
Versailles for Sunday. The great man declared that he had been
keeping that day free in order to arrange his notes, but that he
could not resist the pressing, the almost tender, invitation of his
lovely neighbour.

"Then we'll all of us meet at one o'clock, Sunday, at the Trianon-Palace."

In a weak little voice, Edith said: "I don't think I shall be free."

Madame Tziegel observed that when it was a question of pleasure, one could always be free. She regarded it as a matter for pride that she had once cancelled a private audience at the Vatican. . . . Edith said nothing. Though she appeared to be hesitating, she knew, in her heart of hearts that she would yield. Hurriedly she accumulated a number of reasons for changing her mind. It would be quite idiotic to go dashing off on the strength of a letter, in obedience to the mere whim of an intolerable young man, even supposing it *wasn't* just one of his favourite tricks. He had always loved to feel that he could keep people on a string and move them about as he wished 'Like a little fool, I was going to walk straight into the trap.' Edith had the gift of never seeing things except in the distorting mirror of immediate necessity. Though it had never occurred to her, when Edward's letter had come, not to take it seriously, that was because, at the time, she had welcomed a touch of drama. It had arrived just as she was feeling that she was "on the shelf". But now, in her blissful after-dinner mood, she saw the whole thing as a deliberate piece of mystification. Even though a presentiment of tragedy *did* give her an uncomfortable feeling about the heart, instead of driving it away, she forced herself to call it to heel, to look it in the face, to remember than one *must* be hard, that it was no manner of use getting tied up with anybody, that other people are no more than our eternal playthings. Such an attitude, she thought, was in the true Nietzschean vein. Too much champagne always made her philosophize.

Since the bed looked doubtful, Edward had spread towels

on it before lying down. The rainy sky had hastened the coming on of dusk. He could hear the heavy drops falling on tin roofs. The sound of soldiers marching reached him from the street, and, in imagination, he could catch that smell of leather, polish and human bodies which is peculiar to armies. That he might forget the look of the room he smoked a cigarette impregnated with opium. Nobody would come. He knew that now, and felt neither astonishment nor regret. He felt that he was living in an inaccessible place which no human being would ever succeed in reaching. He determined to bury himself in days that were dead and gone, to escape from life by hiding away in the thickets of the past, so that when death did come he should have gone a considerable distance to meet it. Indifferent now to everything, and already within the shadow of the grave, he felt the memories of his earliest childhood sucking him down like a bog. The mingled stench of cigarette-smoke, dirty curtains, bedside table and slop-pail, was intolerable. But the will to death had freed him from the sensations which once had played too large a part in his responses. To have made up our mind to die is to loosen, by anticipation, all life's hold on us. Nevertheless, he rummaged in his past to find one cool corner, one stretch of green on which to rest his eyes. He tried to fix and hold one single happy minute. He remembered the friendships of his youth, conjured up faces, and was amazed to realize how endlessly ready he had been to let himself be upset by the most wretched of human beings, the shallowest of women. He had never wholly disbelieved in his power to transform, to remould nearer to the heart's desire, the people on whom he had fixed his affections. Though he had fought, unhappily but with determination, to defend against reality the imagined beauties which the loved one had been chiefly instrumental in destroying, too frequent disappointment had had a hardening effect upon him. With a feeling of curiosity he could even bring himself to look within to where his vices lay concealed. He could recognize them, could look them in the eyes, even that one in particular the name of which he had not ever spoken, and that other, too, the very presence of which he had never admitted to himself, a seed deeply buried, unrecognized even by his own heart. How clearly now he could see within himself, could stare into the depths now tragically revealed. He recalled how sudden flashes of confession by those closest to him, had revealed the same abysses in himself, and even depths more terrifying still. That was why he had never felt surprised that he should show, and feel, indulgence for every variant of debauchery, whether admitted or concealed. No time for hypocrisy now that he was face to face with the black density of death, now that he was standing on the threshold of that sleep from which there is no awakening, but utter nothingness. He spoke the last word half aloud: its flavour in his mouth was lovely. He was filled with a sense of dizzy, gentle, falling.

He thought of the dead whom he had loved. Would it make him happy to think, with Christians, that he would meet them once again? No, as perishable beings he had loved them, and in their perishable shapes, sometimes, perhaps, for what was worst in them. He set himself to consider all the lives which had run parallel with his own, which had projected themselves into death, and reached, ahead of him, the crumbling shores of nothingness. What mattered those he was leaving behind? He could imagine them already, ageing grotesques. He, who was going to die at twenty-six, who was certain now that he *would* die at twenty-six, could surrender heart and soul to his hatred of, his disgust for, the men and women of middle age, the creatures with paunches and bald heads, and breath that smelt of cigar-smoke, and of something worse which it served to conceal, of the abject complacency, the self-satisfied look of people who had made a success of life, of their eyes in which passions yelped with hunger now that it was too late for them to be satisfied. His thoughts went to the Paris he had loved. He remembered one night in particular, when, seated in a box, he had pressed his lips to a naked shoulder while Nijinsky leaped through an open window into a scenic night. He saw again the Bars that he had known, each with its own peculiar atmosphere, its own peculiar smell, and how each had drawn him at different moments of the night. In one they served an inimitable cocktail, in another there was the living presence of the vice in which it specialized. He remembered the various orchestras, each playing its own type of music, and each succeeding in fanning his passions – the Schubert andante which he had insisted on May playing to him every evening, the Russian refrain which he had tracked down from concert to concert. He remembered the days when his ambition had been fresh and boyish, when he had craved the adoration of the young and the coteries, as well as the applause of the crowd, all the glories of the flesh: evenings when he was eaten up by rage at the thought that he was doing nothing to advance himself. He had wanted to live in millions of hearts. But because he lacked the will-power which could have served his insatiable appetite, and because he knew that he was incapable of providing it with food, because he could not taste the triumph in which so many others found an excuse for living, he had become the accomplice of all the forces of destruction. It occurred to him now that by killing himself he still might linger on in men's memories. He chuckled: 'One must commit suicide,' he thought, 'in order to survive.'

The light of the June Sunday fell on the flowered tables of the Trianon-Palace. The orchestra was playing just softly enough not to drown the voice of Gennaro who was reciting one of his poems in a low voice. The heads of the assembled guests, all attention, were leaning towards the poet, like the heads of the Apostles in da Vinci's *Last Supper*. Through the French windows Edith could see an avenue of majestic elms, a stranger to this joy, creating for her the streets of that Chalons where she had never been, the hotel bedroom which she could imagine in its every detail and which resembled no room through which she had ever passed. She could see Edward lying on the bed: was he asleep or sick? – how could she know? A tiny fragment of her love came back to her, the love of a woman who was older, stronger than the man she loved. She remembered how she used to call him "little man", and how he was calling to her now, begging her to keep him from dying.

Gennaro stopped speaking. Everyone was trying to think of the right thing to say. One of the ladies declared that for two pins she could have cried. Madame Tziegel made haste to finish her ice. They had sat down to luncheon very late, and the servants were lowering the sun-blinds. Cars were beginning to throb gently in front of the hotel steps.

There would be no point in starting now, thought Edith. Had not Edward fixed on this very Sunday night as the last possible moment? But might it not be possible for her to reach Chalons in the course of the night, or, at least in the early hours of the morning, before he should finally have made up his mind? She was filled with joy to think that she could feel so upset, to know, suddenly, that she was not a monster. There were still some strawberries on her plate. She got up, explained that she had an urgent appointment, and glided away between the tables. Before she had reached the door she could hear stifled laughter behind her. Madame Tziegel was remarking that Edith had accustomed them to a greater show of prudence. She used to cover her trail rather better than this! Who was the man? One only hurries away like that when a first meeting has surpassed all expectation, and a second one is due. Since Jacques Berbinot was the only one who did not laugh, and, like Edith had left his strawberries on his plate, those present felt that it was time to change the conversation.

XVII

C LAUDE struggled out of a sleep which had been full of nightmares. He was burning with fever. What room was this? The early sunlight of a summer's morning was streaming through heart-shaped holes cut in the shutters. The cries of swallows were all about this unknown house. Suddenly he remembered the efforts he had made to break down the door which his father had bolted, his escape by the window, his midnight clamber over the roofs, how, sliding down one of the wooden supports of the barn, and thinking himself closer to the ground than he was, he had dropped, and dropped clumsily. How, he had thought, could he reach Toulenne with a twisted ankle? But he had managed somehow, and, just as dawn was breaking, had reached the first houses of the little town, and gone to an inn where he was not known. He had had scarcely strength enough left to ask for a bowl of hot coffee. He had told the hostess that he had come in from the country to buy a cow, and had twisted his ankle on the way there. She had offered him a bed, and he had decided to rest until it was time to catch the evening train. He had not dared to ask to see the doctor, who knew the Favereau family, and had himself applied a compress to his foot. About four o'clock he had woken up, drunk a little soup, and once more relapsed into a heavy, feverish sleep. He had lost all sense of time. Evening came and the sound of laughter reached him from the bar. He heard the click of billiard balls. In his condition of hazy consciousness he had seen two arms outstretched, a face of utter misery, and Edward's head buried in a pillow. There was blood on the fair hair. . . . He dreamed that he was in the train . . . it was carrying him towards Chalons . . . the movement lulled him. Now at last he could sleep in peace.

He awoke in a panic, thinking of all the hours he had lost. The countryside was loud with the crowing of cocks. The hostess, who had heard him moaning, came in with a bowl of *café-au-lait*. Claude, looking worn and haggard, asked her what day it was.

"Why, Saturday to be sure, market-day."

Saturday! At all costs he had got to reach Chalons by the next evening! He tried to get up. His ankle felt better, but he was shaking with fever. He washed hurriedly. The hostess, who was just off to market, took him with her in the trap, and agreed to drop him at the station. If only he did not run into his father! But all was well: there was no sign of Favereau. Still, he could not avoid having to talk to the woman at the paper-stall, and shaking hands with the Station Master. He explained that he was going into Bordeaux to see a doctor. A porter settled him into a carriage. The train was a slow one, and he now found himself repeating, in the reverse direction, the journey he had made just twelve months earlier. How excited, how full of confidence he had been then! To-day he did not so much as look out of the windows.

At Bordeaux he dragged himself to the booking-office, took his ticket, and sat down on a bench in the waiting-room. It would be several hours before the train started. He did not feel hungry. His body was burning hot, and he was afraid that he might faint. The temptation to sleep was strong, almost

irresistible. It was as though an intolerable weight were lying
on his eyelids. He fought against it: it would be time enough to
sleep when he was in the train. To keep himself awake he
went to the buffet and drank a glass of rum, to sick it up almost
at once in the lavatory. Porters pushing luggage barrows broke
up the groups of waiting travellers. The ground trembled as
an enormous, black goods-train ambled into the station, and
came to a stop. Claude sat with his elbows on his knees and his
head between his hands. It was not until seven o'clock that the
Paris express was made up. He collapsed into a corner seat,
ceased to struggle against his longing for sleep, and lost consciousness. Other people got in. Packets of food were opened.
The mingled smell of sausage and orange-peel made him feel
so ill that he had to open the window. Someone complained of
the cold. The jarring stops jerked him from his nightmare. At
Poitiers, two Sisters of Saint-Vincent-de-Paul sat down opposite.
They looked at him. The elder of the two asked whether he
were feeling ill. The other occupants of the carriage who, up
till then, had taken no notice of him, were sympathetic. The
younger Sister had some aspirin in her basket and made him
swallow two tablets. At Saint-Pierre-les-Corps, though the
buffet was shut, she went off and returned with a cup of hot
milk. He felt less lost in the shelter of these immaculate wings,
and slept more peacefully.

A fresh stop awakened him. He felt much better. The sun
rose over the monotonous landscape of La Beauce. There was
no station in sight. Somebody said that there had been a break-
down. A few of the travellers got out. The train was waiting
for a relief engine from Aubrais. They would be at least three
hours late. Claude took a crumpled time-table from his
pocket. His trembling finger stopped at the word Chalons.
They would miss the connection: he was quite certain that he
was fated to miss it. By the time the train began to move again,

the die had been cast. No power in the world could prevent him from arriving too late.

"How are you feeling, sir?" asked the Sister. The way in which she shook her head showed her that the young man's answer made her distinctly uneasy:

"I am quite all right now: there is no longer any need for me to be ill."

Claude identified the Hôtel de la Cloche while he was still some distance away, because at this early morning hour the front door was open, and a little group of hotel servants was anxiously gathered on the pavement. The moment he got inside, he asked for Edward Dupont-Gunther. The manageress, in a dressing-gown, with a thin rat's-tail of hair hanging down her back, descended the stairs.

"Are you one of the relatives, sir?" Her face brightened. There would be no difficulty now about the formalities, and she need not be worried about the bill.

"I am a friend: I got a letter warning me what might happen. Am I too late?"

"He is still alive, sir; but he has not been moved. The doctor has dressed the wound. Such a nice-looking young gentleman, too! I understand there is no hope. The bullet was deflected but the brain has been injured. I was just getting into bed when I heard the report. Round about midnight it was. My husband said: "Someone in the house has fired a revolver!" – he was too frightened to get up, so it was I who. . . ."

Claude broke in to ask the number of the room and the floor. No one was with him when he went up. Yesterday, he thought, Edward trod these squalid stairs for the last time. He stopped outside the door, then pulled himself together and went in. The first thing he saw was a white bandage which covered Edward's head and part of his face. From under it, two large, wide-open eyes were staring at him. A querulous, childish voice, which he had difficulty in recognizing, broke the silence.

"What's the matter? what's happened? I suppose I'm at Lur, since you're here."

Edward's chest rose and fell. Hair had sprouted round the bloodless lips. At last, Claude managed to speak:

"So I'm not too late: you're still alive."

The injured man fumbled with his bandage, turned his head slightly on the pillow with a groan, and revealed a large scarlet stain. He was no longer looking at Claude, but kept on muttering – "what's the matter? what's the matter?" – then, all of a sudden:

"I am dying."

He took Claude's hand and clung to it like a frightened child. He begged him not to go away, to stay with him always. Claude could feel the nails digging into his flesh. Time passed. Edward could see that Claude's lips were moving.

"Claude," he said, "who are you talking to?"

Then he realized that the other was praying. A phrase came to him out of his distant Protestant childhood:

"In Faith is our salvation."

"Faith is repentance, and repentance is love. Would you like to pray?"

He freed his hand from the dying man's grip. Then he joined Edward's fingers, and, in a loud voice, speaking each word separately and clearly, recited the Lord's Prayer, which Edward repeated after him. When it was over, the man on the bed spoke again:

"There is nobody. . . ."

Very quietly his voice began to ramble. A doctor came in with some ice and a rubber skull-cap. He said that in Paris they would have tried trepanning. Edward did not appear to be in pain. An hour passed. The sound of voices rose from the floor below. There were footsteps in the corridor. Claude opened the door a few inches, and saw in the half light a man who said very quickly:

"Excuse me: I represent the *Chalons-Journal*."

Claude shut the door. A moment later, the manageress appeared, and drew the young man with her into a corner of the room. She had thought it just as well, though the end had not come yet, to get in touch with an undertaker. The Police Superintendant had already been round. There would have to be an enquiry, after which the body could be moved . . . she need not explain, need she? that in an hotel. . . . No doubt the family would wish the body to be taken to Bordeaux. The undertaker would see to everything.

She had raised her voice. No sound of breathing came from the dying man. When she had finished speaking a terrifying silence filled the room. Claude went back to the bed. Never again would Edward's eyes look out upon this world.

Claude had sent a telegram to Firmin Pacaud. The reply, when it came, shocked him. Bertie Dupont-Gunther did not wish to see his son. May was in a very exhausted condition – no doubt the early stages of pregnancy. Business would make it impossible for Firmin Pacaud to come. The family relied on Claude to take all necessary steps, and to arrange for the body to be put in a coffin and sent to Bordeaux. A telegraphed money-order followed. They were quite sure that he would see to everything being done properly.

The shutters were half closed, the window was open. The day promised to be very hot. The sooner the coffin arrived, the better. Claude could not be quite certain whether that slight smell was just imagination. . . . A piece of gauze had been laid on the face and over the waxy hands, because of the flies.

The manageress kept on asking him "to get the room cleared as soon as possible". These mournful details occupied the young man to the exclusion of all other thoughts. There was a step in the corridor, the rustle of a dress. The manageress again, no doubt. But the lady who entered the room seemed at first to Claude a complete stranger. She was wearing a khaki-coloured travelling coat, very narrow in the skirt, and fastened with a single button. Her hat was of the turban type, and her whole appearance that of the odalisque-woman of 1914. It was Edith Gonzales. She took Claude's hand with a little quiver of emotion, and heaved a deep sigh: "If only I had known!" she said, went over to the bed, fell to her knees, quite distinctly murmured the word "forgive", and, finally, burst into tears.

Claude was amazed. Was *this* the woman for whose sake his young master had died? He clenched his fists, then shrugged his shoulders. No, at most Edith had been a pretext sought by a miserable man to justify his yielding to a mood of sudden hopelessness. He had been seized with dizziness, and had fallen from a great height. At the last moment, in a desperate effort to save himself, he had clung to this branch, but it had snapped off short. But so would any other branch have done under the weight of his despair.

The woman's every gesture seemed to him to be studied and false. For all that, Edith's tears were perfectly genuine. She lifted a corner of the gauze, leaned over the body, but almost at once recoiled, not so much because of the cotton wads in the nostrils and the bandage supporting the jaw, as because the face was unrecognizable. The man who lay before her had, all of a sudden, become a total stranger. Eternal peace had smoothed the face which to her had never expressed anything but unhappiness and bewilderment. This was what the poor boy ought to have been, could have been. Claude, too, had moved to the bed. He was conscious of a similar shock, and said:

"One has only to look at a friend when he is dead to understand that one has never really known him."

In spite of the heat in this dark, malodorous room, Edith began to shiver. She was frightened, a prey to that instinctive repulsion which seizes on dumb animals at the entrance to the slaughterhouse.

With a note of pleading in her voice, she said:

"There's nothing more I can do here, is there?"

She was begging for permission to run away.

"You don't need me any longer?"

Of the two of them, only Claude tried to pray. The looking-glass of the wardrobe door, and its smaller fellow over the washstand, multiplied the rigid figure on the bed. It was as though the room were filled with a hecatomb of young men. The heat was becoming unbearable. 1914 promised to be a wonderful year for wine, better even than 1911. Heavy footsteps sounded on the stairs. Outside the door men could be heard breathing heavily under the weight of the leaden box they were carrying on their shoulders.

Just outside Paris the express came to a stop. Edith looked at the June haze above the house-tops. A savage craving for happiness made her feel ashamed, disgusted. She drove from her mind, like a fly, something that Madame Gonzales had whispered in her ear the previous evening. It has been obsessing her.

"When a man kills himself for a woman, my pet, her fortune is made."

FINE WORKS OF FICTION
AVAILABLE IN QUALITY
PAPERBACK EDITIONS FROM
CARROLL & GRAF

☐ Asch, Sholem/THE APOSTLE — $10.95
☐ Asch, Sholem/MARY — $10.95
☐ Asch, Sholem/THE NAZARENE — $10.95
☐ Asch, Sholem/THREE CITIES — $10.50
☐ Ashley, Mike (ed.)/THE MAMMOTH BOOK OF SHORT HORROR NOVELS — $8.95
☐ Asimov, Isaac/THE MAMMOTH BOOK OF CLASSIC SCIENCE FICTION (1930s) — $8.95
☐ Asimov, Isaac et al/THE MAMMOTH BOOK OF GOLDEN AGE SCIENCE FICTION (1940) — $8.95
☐ Babel, Isaac/YOU MUST KNOW EVERYTHING — $8.95
☐ Balzac, Honore de/BEATRIX — $8.95
☐ Balzac, Honoré de/CESAR BIROTTEAU — $8.95
☐ Balzac, Honoré de/THE LILY OF THE VALLEY — $9.95
☐ Bellaman, Henry/KINGS ROW — $8.95
☐ Bernanos, George/DIARY OF A COUNTRY PRIEST — $7.95
☐ Brand, Christianna/GREEN FOR DANGER — $8.95
☐ Céline, Louis-Ferdinand/CASTLE TO CASTLE — $8.95
☐ Chekov, Anton/LATE BLOOMING FLOWERS — $8.95
☐ Conrad, Joseph/SEA STORIES — $8.95
☐ Conrad, Joseph & Ford Madox Ford/ THE INHERITORS — $7.95
☐ Conrad, Joseph & Ford Madox Ford/ROMANCE — $8.95
☐ Coward, Noel/A WITHERED NOSEGAY — $8.95
☐ de Montherlant, Henry/THE GIRLS — $11.95
☐ Dos Passos, John/THREE SOLDIERS — $9.95
☐ Feuchtwanger, Lion/JEW SUSS — $8.95
☐ Feuchtwanger, Lion/THE OPPERMANNS — $8.95
☐ Fisher, R.L./THE PRINCE OF WHALES — $5.95
☐ Fitzgerald, Penelope/OFFSHORE — $7.95
☐ Fitzgerald, Penelope/INNOCENCE — $7.95
☐ Flaubert, Gustave/NOVEMBER — $7.95
☐ Fonseca, Rubem/HIGH ART — $7.95
☐ Fuchs, Daniel/SUMMER IN WILLIAMSBURG — $8.95

- [ ] Gold, Michael/JEWS WITHOUT MONEY   **$7.95**
- [ ] Greenberg & Waugh (eds.)/THE NEW
  ADVENTURES OF SHERLOCK HOLMES   **$8.95**
- [ ] Greene, Graham & Hugh/THE SPY'S BEDSIDE
  BOOK   **$7.95**
- [ ] Greenfeld, Josh/THE RETURN OF MR.
  HOLLYWOOD   **$8.95**
- [ ] Hamsun, Knut/MYSTERIES   **$8.95**
- [ ] Hardinge, George (ed.)/THE MAMMOTH BOOK
  OF MODERN CRIME STORIES   **$8.95**
- [ ] Hawkes, John/VIRGINIE: HER TWO LIVES   **$7.95**
- [ ] Higgins, George/TWO COMPLETE NOVELS   **$9.95**
- [ ] Hugo, Victor/NINETY-THREE   **$8.95**
- [ ] Huxley, Aldous/ANTIC HAY   **$10.95**
- [ ] Huxley, Aldous/EYELESS IN GAZA   **$9.95**
- [ ] Ibañez, Vincente Blasco/THE FOUR HORSEMEN
  OF THE APOCALYPSE   **$8.95**
- [ ] Jackson, Charles/THE LOST WEEKEND   **$7.95**
- [ ] James, Henry/GREAT SHORT NOVELS   **$12.95**
- [ ] Jones, Richard Glyn/THE MAMMOTH BOOK
  OF MURDER   **$8.95**
- [ ] Lewis, Norman/DAY OF THE FOX   **$8.95**
- [ ] Lowry, Malcolm/HEAR US O LORD FROM
  HEAVEN THY DWELLING PLACE   **$9.95**
- [ ] Lowry, Malcolm/ULTRAMARINE   **$7.95**
- [ ] Macaulay, Rose/CREWE TRAIN   **$8.95**
- [ ] Macaulay, Rose/KEEPING UP APPEARANCES   **$8.95**
- [ ] Macaulay, Rose/DANGEROUS AGES   **$8.95**
- [ ] Macaulay, Rose/THE TOWERS OF
  TREBIZOND   **$8.95**
- [ ] Mailer, Norman/BARBARY SHORE   **$9.95**
- [ ] Mauriac, François/THE DESERT OF LOVE   **$6.95**
- [ ] Mauriac, François/FLESH AND BLOOD   **$8.95**
- [ ] Mauriac, François/WOMAN OF THE
  PHARISEES   **$8.95**
- [ ] Mauriac, François/VIPER'S TANGLE   **$8.95**
- [ ] McElroy, Joseph/THE LETTER LEFT TO ME   **$7.95**
- [ ] McElroy, Joseph/LOOKOUT CARTRIDGE   **$9.95**
- [ ] McElroy, Joseph/PLUS   **$8.95**
- [ ] McElroy, Joseph/A SMUGGLER'S BIBLE   **$9.50**
- [ ] Moorcock, Michael/THE BROTHEL IN
  ROSENTRASSE   **$6.95**
- [ ] Munro, H.H./THE NOVELS AND PLAYS OF
  SAKI   **$8.95**

☐	Neider, Charles (ed.)/GREAT SHORT STORIES	$11.95
☐	Neider, Charles (ed.)/SHORT NOVELS OF THE MASTERS	$12.95
☐	O'Faolain, Julia/THE OBEDIENT WIFE	$7.95
☐	O'Faolain, Julia/NO COUNTRY FOR YOUNG MEN	$8.95
☐	O'Faolain, Julia/WOMEN IN THE WALL	$8.95
☐	Olinto, Antonio/THE WATER HOUSE	$9.95
☐	Plievier, Theodore/STALINGRAD	$8.95
☐	Pronzini & Greenberg (eds.)/THE MAMMOTH BOOK OF PRIVATE EYE NOVELS	$8.95
☐	Rechy, John/BODIES AND SOULS	$8.95
☐	Rechy, John/MARILYN'S DAUGHTER	$8.95
☐	Rhys, Jean/QUARTET	$6.95
☐	Sand, George/MARIANNE	$7.95
☐	Scott, Evelyn/THE WAVE	$9.95
☐	Sigal, Clancy/GOING AWAY	$9.95
☐	Singer, I.J./THE BROTHERS ASHKENAZI	$9.95
☐	Taylor, Peter/IN THE MIRO DISTRICT	$7.95
☐	Tolstoy, Leo/TALES OF COURAGE AND CONFLICT	$11.95
☐	van Thal, Herbert/THE MAMMOTH BOOK OF GREAT DETECTIVE STORIES	$8.95
☐	Wassermann, Jacob/CASPAR HAUSER	$9.95
☐	Wassermann, Jabob/THE MAURIZIUS CASE	$9.95
☐	Werfel, Franz/THE FORTY DAYS OF MUSA DAGH	$9.95
☐	Winwood, John/THE MAMMOTH BOOK OF SPY THRILLERS	$8.95

Available from fine bookstores everywhere or use this coupon for ordering.

Carroll & Graf Publishers, Inc., 260 Fifth Avenue, N.Y., N.Y. 10001

Please send me the books I have checked above. I am enclosing $_____ (please add $1.00 per title to cover postage and handling.) Send check or money order—no cash or C.O.D.'s please. N.Y. residents please add 8¼% sales tax.

Mr/Mrs/Ms _____

Address _____

City _____ State/Zip _____

Please allow four to six weeks for delivery.